TAKE HER

Andrew
I hope you enjoy
the story!

Tara White

TARA WHITE

Take Her
Copyright © 2020 by Tara White

Tellwell Talent
www.tellwell.ca

ISBN
978-0-2288-4427-3 (Hardcover)
978-0-2288-4426-6 (Paperback)
978-0-2288-4428-0 (eBook)

This book is dedicated to my partner Mark and my family.
Thank you for always believing in me.

PROLOGUE

*O*w, I thought, as I started to wake from a deep sleep. I shifted under my blanket and rubbed my sore belly. I tried to sit up, but a pain shot across my stomach, so I stayed down. I buried my face in my blanket and held both arms across my stomach while I pushed down on my belly to try to make the pain go away.

"Mommy!" I called. My voice cracked, still scratchy with sleep. "Mommy!" I called again. I tried to be loud enough to wake my mom, but quiet enough so that I didn't wake my sister, who was sound asleep in the bunk above me.

As I lay there, I held my breath and listened, hoping to hear my mom walking toward my bedroom. Instead, tears filled my eyes as the sound of silence echoed loudly through my mind. I squeezed my eyes shut and a single tear escaped. I wiped it from my cheek as I rolled over, still wrapped in my blanket, and slid softly off my mattress, trying hard to move slowly so the bed wouldn't creak too much. I pulled my pink-and-yellow comforter off me and shoved it on my bed in a crumpled heap.

The tiara that I wore everywhere fell out of the blanket as I tossed it. It always fell off while I slept. I picked it up and put it back on my head. It was just a cheap one; I got it at the dollar store when Mommy said I could pick out anything I wanted and I'd worn it every day since.

I stood still and listened to make sure I hadn't woken up my sister. When I heard her steady breathing, I tiptoed across the room, careful not to step on the toys that were all over the floor, and out the door.

The house was quiet, too quiet. There was always a lot of noise in our house, lots of music and talking and laughing. The only time it was quiet was in the middle of the night, after everyone was asleep. I continued to tiptoe through the house and stepped over a body that was sprawled out, asleep on the living room floor.

The smell of coffee drifted from the kitchen. I snuck quietly past the doorway and jumped when my mom yelled, "Ah, shit."

I looked back as she grabbed a dish towel and wiped spilled coffee off her arm. I turned, continued to the front door and grabbed my sneakers. I was just about done tying the second one when I heard my mom. "Where are you going?" she asked as she held a mug up to her lips and took a sip. Steam from the coffee fogged her glasses and made her eyes disappear.

"To the park," I answered.

"Take your sister," she mumbled.

"I just want to go by myself for once," I whined. "I'm not feeling good."

"Then you shouldn't be going to the park," she said.

"I'm not that bad," I said, changing my story so I wouldn't be stuck there. "I just need to pee, then I'll feel better."

"So pee already and take your sister with you," she repeated.

"I don't want to," I complained. "I always have to take her."

"Take her with you or stay home," Mom said and took another sip from her mug.

"Fine," I grumbled and kicked off my shoes. "Who's that?" I asked, pointing to the sleeping body that I had stepped over.

"Daddy's friend. Now come give me a kiss," she said, reaching her arms out to me when I walked by.

I pretended to try to avoid her. She reached for me, grabbed my arm and pulled me into a big bear hug as she kissed the top of my head. She wobbled, and I felt her weight lean against me as she used me to hold herself up. I shifted slightly as her hot mug rested against my arm. "Are you feeling better today?" I asked hopefully. "Can you take us to the park?"

"Not today, honey," she said. "I'm just not feeling right. Go with your sister, you'll be fine."

"Listen to your mother," Daddy said from the couch.

"Fine," I sulked and headed back to my room. The man asleep on the floor grumbled and rolled over onto his back as I passed.

Our bunk bed wobbled and squeaked as I climbed the ladder and called to my sister. The bed creaked loudly, complaints echoing from the old ladder rungs as my weight shifted with each step. "Come on," I said, shaking her leg.

My sister stirred but did not open her eyes.

"Let's go," I said, shaking her harder. She didn't move so I pinched her. "Get up."

"Ow," she complained, sitting up to grab her calf where I pinched her. "Where are we going?" she asked, rubbing her brown eyes with little fists. Her long dark hair poked out from behind her head, where I was sure she had another huge knot. It didn't matter how many times a day I brushed her hair, it was always full of knots.

"To the park."

"I'm tired, I don't want to go."

"Too bad," I said, tugging on her pyjama sleeve. "Mommy said I have to take you."

I started tickling her belly until she finally squealed. "Okay, I'm getting up."

I picked out clothes for her and helped her get dressed, pulling a sweater over her head at the last second. On the way out, she tripped over the sleeping body and fell on her knees. Before she could cry, I ran over to her and helped her up. Then I put on her shoes, fastening the Velcro straps up tight. I looked back and saw

Daddy handing some medicine over to Mommy before we headed out the door.

I ran ahead, staying a few steps in front of her as she struggled to keep up. She was little, so she couldn't run very fast. I knew that if I stayed in front of her she would run as fast as she could to try to catch me. It was a foggy and cool morning, which made me shiver and wish I had grabbed a sweater for myself.

I was happy that I had picked out a sweater for her at least, thinking that she didn't look cold at all as I stopped at the edge of the park to wait for her. "Push me," she yelled as she ran past me to the swing set. She climbed into a swing, sending a flock of birds flapping away as they squawked at her in complaint. She sat there, scissor-kicking her feet and squirming in the swing as she waited for me.

I pushed through the fog, which was thick all around us. It floated like a dirty cloud through the park, making it seem a little spooky.

"Pump your legs," I said as I pushed her, "then you can keep yourself going."

"But I like it better when you push me," she said, her legs dangling lifelessly below her. She leaned back, arms stretched out, her tiny fists squeezing the chains. Her eyes were closed, and she had a huge smile on her face. Her long, ratty hair brushed the sand as she swung back and forth.

"Higher!" she shouted.

I pushed her for a while as she swung happily. "That's enough," I said after I got bored. "Let's go on the slide now."

The main part of the playground was empty, as it usually was when we came here this early. I watched as she jumped off the swing and fell in the sand. She picked up a handful of sand and threw it onto the grass. Then she scurried up and ran to a patch of dandelions, kneeling in front of them as she plucked them from their roots, sending drops of dew flying as she gathered them in her fist.

"Get up," I said. "Your pants are going to get all wet."

She just shrugged and pulled up some more dandelions.

At the far edge of the park, there was an old woman walking a little black-and-white dog. I'd seen her before, so I waved to her and she waved back before she continued walking her dog, who kept its nose to the ground, sniffing as it walked.

At the other end there was a man standing at the edge of the forest that bordered the park. It looked like he was watching us, but when I waved to him, he just turned his back to us. Birds chirped happily from the forest, calling to people, telling them to get out and enjoy the day. I was happy no one was listening to them. I didn't want to share the playground with anyone. I wanted us to be alone.

"For you," she said, shoving the fistful of weeds into my face, pulling my attention away from the man near the forest.

"Thanks," I said, taking them from her. "Here, look," I said. I pulled one dandelion from the bunch and held it, placing my thumb underneath the flower. "Mama had a baby and her head popped off." I flicked my thumb and sent the yellow top flying.

She bent over and held her belly, giggling with delight. When she stood back up her cheeks were red and her eyes were sparkling. "Again, again," she laughed.

I sang the song again and sent another yellow top soaring. After another burst of giggles her smile disappeared and she looked like she was going to cry.

"Did Mama's head pop off when she had me?" Her bottom lip pushed out and her eyes went wide.

"Don't be stupid," I said. "It's just a song for dandelions."

"Oh, okay," she said, looking relieved.

"You ready to slide now?" I asked and threw the handful of weeds down.

My sister followed me and we laughed as we ran up the stairs and slid quickly down the windy slide. We soaked up the layer of water beads on the surface with our pants as we slid down. We kicked off our shoes and socks after the third trip down. The playground was so colourful and happy, with two bright yellow slides, one windy, one straight, dark red steps and a neon green fireman pole. Seeing all the bright colours always made me feel happy inside.

"Let's make a train," I said and sat at the top of the straight slide, waiting for her to catch up and climb in behind me. She slid her legs down around me and I grabbed her feet, pulling them up over my thighs. She threw her arms around my neck. "Too tight," I complained, pulling her hands apart to loosen her hold on my neck. "Like this," I said, moving her hands down so they wrapped around my belly instead. "Ready? One. Two. Three. Let's go!" I shouted and pushed off.

"Wee!" she squealed into my ear.

At the bottom I dug my bare feet into the sand, wiggling my toes as the cool sand moved between them. Then I noticed the shoes of someone standing on the grass, just past where the sand ended. I looked up and was surprised to see a man standing there. It was the man from the edge of the forest. He was wearing jogging pants and a blue sweatshirt that had dark stains on it around the neck and under his arms. His dark hair was wavy and curled up at the base of his neck. He brushed his bangs, wet with sweat, out of his eyes.

We climbed off the slide and stood there, staring at him, my sister behind me, arms around my belly, as she leaned over to peek around me.

I looked around the park; the old woman with the dog was gone. No one else was there.

"Are you girls here all alone?" the man asked, looking around nervously.

I nodded.

"Well," the man said, smiling. "That's very interesting." He brushed his bangs from his eyes again as a bead of sweat dripped down his forehead.

"You girls are very pretty," he said. "You look so much alike. How old are you?"

"I'm five," I said.

"I'm three," my sister said, as she peeked out from behind me again and held up three pudgy little fingers.

"Where are your parents?" he asked.

"Asleep at home," I answered.

He smiled again and I recognized him. I had seen him at the park before, many times, watching us.

"That's very interesting," he said again, rubbing his forehead. "I tell you what," he continued, rubbing his hands together, "I can only take one of you home with me right now. And you," he said, pointing at me, "are going to decide which one of you that will be."

Without thinking, I knew what I had to do. I tugged my sister out from behind me and moved her around me until we had switched places, me behind her with my hands on her shoulders.

"Take her," I said, and gave her shoulders a little shove forward.

CHAPTER 1

Danica

I brush my teeth and put on my pyjamas, like a good girl, like I've been told to do. I don't want to make anyone mad, so I try to follow all the rules. But there are so many, I can't always remember all of them. I always remember to brush my teeth, though, because the one night I forgot, I got pulled out of bed by my hair and had to brush my teeth with hot water while they stood and watched. The steam from the running tap water had burned my nostrils as I breathed it in, and my gums burned from the scalding hot water on my toothbrush. It was my own fault that they had to teach me a lesson. Dental hygiene is important. I learned my lesson that night, and I'll never forget it.

Music is blaring from the living room and I hear people laughing and bottles clinking as I walk back to my room with my dirty clothes rolled into a ball in my arms. I step into my bedroom, toss the clothes toward the hamper in the corner, and jump into bed. As I fluff up my pillow, I see the clothes have missed the hamper. I quickly hop back out of bed and move them to the hamper. I must take care of my stuff and keep my room clean. That's another lesson I've learned well. I notice a dust ball in the corner, so I scoop that up and tuck it down into the hamper with the clothes.

The bass from the music rattles the floor behind my feet. *Party time*, I think with a shudder so hard it literally makes my entire body shake. I hear at least three different voices talking and laughing, but there could be more. I push my door closed, drowning out some of the noise from the living room and am headed back to my bed when I hear a bottle shatter on the floor and then a burst of laughter.

"Danny! Danny, get down here!" someone yells from downstairs.

I ignore it and climb into my bed.

"Now, Danny!" The voice is Benson's. It's serious, and angry.

I get back out of bed and move quickly across my room and down the stairs. I almost step in the broken glass that's shattered on the living room floor.

"It's Danica," I say, crossing my arms as I stare at them with a scowl on my face.

"Whatever. Clean this up for us," Benson says. He's sitting on the couch and pointing to the broken glass. He brushes his other hand through his long, greasy hair, then wipes his palm on his thigh, adding another stain to his sweat-stained clothes. He's always sweaty, even though all he ever does is sit on the couch and drink beer. He buries his hand into a bag of potato chips and pulls out a handful. He shoves them in his mouth, dropping bits of chips all over his shirt.

"You tell her, Benny." Another guy, sitting across from them on a smaller couch laughs as he raises his beer then takes a big sip. He's really skinny with short blond hair and a moustache. He's wearing jeans and a white undershirt so that I can see his hairy armpit when he lifts his arm. He's been here before; I remember him. When he puts the bottle down beside five other bottles, he looks right at me and licks his lips slowly, catching a few drops of beer stuck in his moustache with his tongue. All the hairs on the back of my neck stand up.

"But I'm tired," I complain. "Can I clean it up in the morning, Crystal?" I ask, turning to the woman on the couch beside Benson. She's holding a bottle of beer to her lips and drinks half the bottle in one sip. Her blond, curly hair is in a messy ponytail off to the side and loose strands of hair are dancing out around her face. She's wearing a tight tank top, one strap dangling down around her upper arm and a blanket draped across her lap. Her bare feet, with pink painted toenails, are peeking out from under the blanket.

"Mom," the woman snaps, "how many times do I have to tell you to call me Mom and him Dad," she snarls, pointing at Benson with her chin. He's shoving another fistful of chips into his mouth. Her eyes are only half open as she looks at me and her blue eyes are almost crossed. I'm sure she doesn't even really see me as she looks toward me. Her makeup is all messy, reminding me of a scary clown I saw in a horror movie once that I watched when she wasn't home. I had been so happy when Benson had said I was old enough to watch it, but then I was so scared afterwards that I had nightmares for a week.

"I'm tired, Mom," I say, emphasizing the last word.

"Too bad," Benson says, "clean it up now."

"Cr . . . Mom, please?" I beg.

"We're having this party to celebrate *your* birthday," she slurs, "so stop being so ungrateful and clean it up for us."

"You remembered my birthday?" I ask. She hadn't mentioned it all day.

"Of course, I remembered," she says. "What kind of mother do you think I am? We got you a cake, baby."

"And Les is paying me double tonight," Benson whispers to me, blocking his mouth with his hand so she doesn't hear him, "being that it's your special day and all." He winks and smiles, baring all his crooked, rotting teeth.

My body jerks and I heave, throwing up in my mouth, but I swallow it back down quickly, so I don't get smacked. Last year

I had the flu and threw up on the rug. I had to take a week off school, not because of the flu, but because I had a dark bruise in the shape of Benson's hand across my face that took a week to disappear. Mom said she didn't want anyone at school to see it because they might get the wrong idea and that would just cause trouble for them that they didn't have time for. She said she didn't want people to start asking questions, "because it wasn't nobody's business what happened in her home."

When I don't move, Benson stands up, sends the bag of chips tumbling to the floor, and takes a step toward me. I flinch when he raises his hand. His armpit has a sweat stain that goes halfway down his side and his greasy hair falls in front of his face. I'm happy that it covers his eyes and I don't have to see him look at me with the mean look he always has. He scares me. "Clean this up now, then you can go to bed," he says.

I move quickly, picking up the biggest pieces of glass in my hands. They are still wet with beer, and slippery, so I cut my finger on a sharp edge. Blood trickles down my finger and a single drop lands on the floor. I put my finger in my mouth to stop the blood and I can taste the beer from the glass pieces. It tastes bad, I don't know why they drink so much of it. I bend and wipe up the blood from the floor with my pyjama sleeve and drop the glass shards in the garbage.

On the counter is a half-eaten cake that says, "Hap Bir Bar." There are fork marks through the remaining letters, crumbs all over the counter and more on the floor. Three forks lie in the crumbs on the counter. The sticker on the plastic cake cover says, "Order Cancelled - Sale $3.99." The sink is piled high with dirty dishes. I don't bother with the dishes—I know they'll still be there in the morning, waiting for me. I'll have to get up early so I can wash them before I leave for school.

I grab paper towel to wipe up the spilled beer and the tiny glass pieces, the ones that are too small to pick up with my fingers. I run a fresh piece of paper towel under the tap and squeeze out the extra water. As I wipe it across the floor to get rid of the stickiness, I look up and see Benson trying to kiss Crystal. She swats him away like he's a pesky mosquito and she flops backwards into the couch, pulling the blanket up over her face.

"I'm tired, Benny," she whines, "leave me alone."

He leans toward her and tries to pull the blanket from her. She kicks at him and gets him in the ribs.

"Bitch," he growls and swats her leg.

"Ooh, ooh, ooh." The second guy laughs. "Looks like you've been told, Benny." He takes another swig of beer.

"Shut up, jackass," Benson says and throws a beer bottle at him. Luckily, it's empty and only a couple of drops fall from it and it flies across the living room. Even luckier, it lodges into the couch cushions, so it doesn't break. The second guy just laughs and raises his beer bottle to his lips again.

My stomach knots. I know what's coming later.

"Can I go now?" I ask.

Benson looks past me, inspecting the spot where the broken bottle had been. "Go!" he growls, and I turn and run up the stairs, taking them two at a time.

I shut my bedroom door quickly behind me. Someone turns up the music and I hear it loudly through my door; the bass from the song is making my floor vibrate beneath my feet. The talking and laughing get louder, too.

I scan my room and I can see a little bit thanks to the moonlight coming in through my window. I open my window and lean far out, looking to the ground at the driveway below. A light snow is falling, and the air is cold. I blow out and watch my breath dance from my lips until it disappears. I wish that I could disappear into thin air also. I stand there for a long time, trying to figure out my chances of making the jump without breaking one or both legs. I finally decide that the odds are not good, and the only thing worse than living here would be living here with broken legs, so I close my window and turn to my next plan.

I lay my pillow across my bed and pull the covers up over it. I arrange a couple of stuffed animals around the pillow. Then I lie on the floor and try to squeeze under the bed. It's getting too tight, and I can't get fully under it anymore, so I wiggle to get myself back out. I look around my room. My stomach knots when I realize there are no good hiding places in here. Even under the bed was lame, but at least it had worked occasionally.

There was no pattern that I had been able to figure out, so I was rarely able to get a good sleep. Sometimes he came into my room at night and sometimes he didn't. Sometimes it was someone else. I didn't know who, I just knew it wasn't Benson. So, I was always on alert—even in sleep, I was always listening for the sound of my doorknob turning long after I had put myself to bed.

What I did know for sure, was that every time they had a party, whether they had one guest or twenty guests, Benson always came looking for me those nights. I had started sleeping under my bed every time I heard the loud music playing.

Sometimes, if he got really drunk, he would just fall over when he tried to bend down to pull me out from under the bed. After a few wobbly swipes of his arm, a few topples over onto his knees, he would swear and kick the bed then disappear out of my room. Those were the few nights when I was able to get some sleep because he had never come back on the same night to try again. I'd stay, tucked safely under my bed, and drift into a wonderful deep sleep, my heart bursting with joy over my small victory. The victory never lasted long, though, and the next day he was always extra mean. His kicks would be harder, his smacks more frequent, his words filled with more poison. It was worth every extra bruise, every harsh insult, to know that I had won, if only for a single night.

If he wasn't too drunk, though, he would keep swiping his arm under the bed until he would catch my leg, or a piece of my pyjamas and pull me out. He didn't care if I cried. He didn't care if he hurt me. He didn't care if I begged him to stop. He didn't care about anything.

Shaking my head to get thoughts of him out of my mind, I decide my only option is the closet. So I open the door, step inside, and pull the door shut behind me, closing out the moon and turning my world instantly black.

I curl up in a corner, behind old toys and dirty clothes that never made it to the hamper. My dresses dangle above me, swinging from their hangers, tickling my neck. I push them out of the way and pull my knees up to my chest. The music pulses through the floor beneath me. I rock myself and squeeze my eyes shut, wishing with all my heart for the wall to swallow me up and take me away from my miserable life.

I pull up a picture in my mind of another little girl, in a different time and place, celebrating her birthdays with cake and ice cream, princesses and presents. I have a memory of her, of a brief time when we were sisters. As much as I loved her, still love her, a small part of me also hates her, because she is the reason I am here and that is something I can never forget.

The music from the living room becomes louder again, pulling me back from my daydreams and I fall asleep to the sound of drunken laughter and clinking beer bottles. I wake up later when I hear the closet doorknob turn. I'm instantly awake and I feel my heart race. It's beating so fast I feel like it's going to pop right out of my shirt. I hold my breath, quiet as a mouse, trying to be invisible while I fight the urge to kick and scream and scratch. I want to fight. I want to hurt him like he hurts me. Instead, fear turns me into a statue. I curse myself for being afraid. I hate myself for not fighting.

"Come out, come out, wherever you are," a scruffy, drunken voice says in a sing-song tone that reminds me of a freakish cartoon character. It's Benson's voice, the sound from all my nightmares.

I feel my clothes swishing around above me on their hangers as his hands dig through my closet, trying to find me. "I know you're in here," he says. I feel him take another step closer. I pull my knees up tighter to my chest just as he finds me.

"Aha!" he says, like an excited child. "Gotcha. Come out, come out, wherever you are," he repeats in his sing-song manner as he wraps a hand around each ankle and quickly yanks me toward him. The back of my head hits the wall as I feel my body pulled out from under me. I slide easily across the floor, my fleece pyjamas slippery against the wood floor. I throw my head backwards against the floor as he pulls me, hoping I'll knock myself out. It fails. I stop suddenly when I slam into him and he laughs. "Ha ha, that's a good girl."

I squirm and try to roll over, but he still has one hand on each ankle. He squeezes tighter and I yelp.

"The more you fight, the more it hurts," he warns, his sloppy words spitting into my face as he speaks.

I turn and wipe his beer-flavoured spit from my face with the back of my hand as he puts his hand on my chin and turns my face back toward him. I hold my breath as I feel his face move closer to mine. "That's my good girl," he moans as I gag from the taste of beer and cigarettes.

"I have a ssssurprise for you for your, your bir— birfday," he says drunkenly as he pulls me the rest of the way out of the closet and lifts me quickly, scooping me off the floor. My body goes limp in his arms. I see the second guy standing in the light of the doorway. He's smiling as he moves one hand inside the front of his jeans. "Les is gonna wish you a haffy birfday when I'm done."

There's no point fighting. I know this. I've learned this. He staggers over to my bed, hits his head and releases me, dropping my limp body onto my mattress. I roll twice until I'm at the end of the mattress, right against the wall. "Son of a bitch," he moans, as he rubs his head. In the moonlight I can see him sway and stagger, and for a moment I am filled with the hope that he'll fall down in a drunken fit and pass out.

But tonight it is not my lucky night. He regains his balance and steadies himself. I turn and tuck my face into the corner and squeeze my eyes shut. I think again of another little girl, with brown eyes and dark hair just like mine. She's smiling, playing in her backyard with a furry little puppy, giggling as the puppy pounces on her and runs around chasing her. I focus on her joy as I feel Benson roll me out of the corner and yank my pyjama bottoms down. I see her bright smile as he puts his mouth over mine again.

Be safe, Elly, I repeat silently to myself as I close my eyes and let my world go black.

CHAPTER 2

Elaina

"Happy birthday, princess!" Mom and Dad shout when I walk through the door.

The lights turn on, blinding me for a moment as a sea of voices yell, "Surprise!" from behind them. As my eyes adjust to the bright light, I see the room is filled with my family and friends. I look through their faces and see my Aunt Sophia and Uncle Victor, my older cousins Karen and Marcy. I run up and hug them because they live so far away that I don't get to see them much. My best friends Jenny and Patricia are here. A bunch of kids from school and from my soccer team are here, too. Both our neighbours are here with their kids.

The room is filled; there are people everywhere talking and laughing. Kids are running around chasing each other. The house is full, but it feels like there is someone missing. I can't figure out who, but as I go through the room, taking turns hugging each person, I realize I'm looking for someone. For a moment I'm startled when I think I've found her, but then I realize it's just the mirror on the far end of the room and it is my own reflection that I see.

So weird, I think, staring at my reflection, trying hard to focus. *Who am I looking for?* It feels like there are snakes in my belly, squirming and wriggling around. It feels yucky.

"Where's the birthday girl?" soft voices call out and I turn to look. Two princesses, a red-haired Ariel and a blond Cinderella walk through the doorway. They twirl and their dresses come alive, dancing around them as they wave their wands and throw glittery confetti up into the air. I watch the confetti as it floats down and lands in a little pool of sparkles around my feet.

"Yay!" I cheer, forgetting about my reflection and clapping my hands together. I love princesses.

I stop clapping when I notice Mommy and Daddy in a corner talking. Mommy looks upset, like she's been crying. She's holding a cup of coffee in both hands and takes a small sip every few seconds. Daddy hugs her and takes the mug from her, placing it down on a little table, then takes her hand and leads her upstairs. She's pulling back on his hand like she doesn't want to go, but he keeps tugging and eventually she gives up and follows him upstairs.

"A present for the birthday girl," Cinderella says, and hands me a wand. "Close your eyes, wave your wand in the air and make a wish," she says and winks at me. I take the wand and close my eyes. *I wish I could be a real princess.*

"We'll be right back," Ariel says, and she and Cinderella leave the room for a moment and return, each of them carrying a handle of a chest.

"Time to turn all of you into little princesses and princes," Cinderella says.

We all scream with delight and race to the chest. "Not you," Ariel says to me. "We have a very special dress just for you," she says, handing me a box topped with a huge pink bow.

I pull the lid off and there is the most beautiful, sparkly dress I've ever seen. I pull it over my clothes, and it fits perfectly. Ariel pulls my long hair up into a bun and adds a few jewelled bobby pins. Then she pulls a brand-new tiara out from behind her back. It is the most beautiful thing I have ever seen. It's covered in diamonds, rubies and emeralds. They look like they're real. She places it on my head, and I feel myself being transformed into a real princess. She tells me to close my eyes as she sprays sparkly glitter into my hair then holds up a mirror to my face.

I don't even recognize my reflection. "I'm a real princess!" I shout and jump into Ariel to hug her.

"Yes, you are," Daddy says, reaching the bottom step alone.

"Where's Mommy?" I ask.

"She's not feeling good," he says, "so I gave her some medicine. She's going to rest for a little bit, and she'll come back down later. He smiles at me and starts clicking the button on his camera. He wipes his hand across his forehead then returns the camera to his face, the flash flickering as he takes picture after picture. "Twirl around," he says. "Let me get a picture of your dress when you spin."

I do as he says and twirl around and around. My dress is flying up around me, making me feel like I'm floating on a cloud. I keep laughing and twirling and hear Daddy's camera clicking as he takes pictures. *This is the best day of my life.*

Ariel and Cinderella lead all the princesses and princes to the basement, which has been decorated with huge fake lilies and daisies and pink balloons. We have a tea party and play games.

"Happy birthday to you," Daddy starts singing and everyone joins in to finish the whole song. He's holding a cake as he walks toward me. The flames on the little candles are dancing around and lighting up his face. I think I have the most handsome daddy in the whole world. He leans down and places the cake in front of me. "Time to make a wish," he says.

I close my eyes and think about my wish. I'm trying to decide whether to wish for a puppy or a new doll when I take a deep breath in and lean toward my cake. As I push out my breath and see the flames on the candles disappear, the only words I think are

I hope I see her again someday. Everyone claps and smiles when all the candles have been blown out. I smile, too, at everyone, but I feel sad inside. *What does my wish even mean?* I wonder.

Daddy cuts up the cake and we all eat cake and ice cream and then I open my presents. There are a lot of presents and it takes forever to open all of them. When I'm done, I'm sitting in a huge pile of ripped-up wrapping paper and ribbons. There are piles of toys, a brand-new dollhouse with a family of dolls, a radio from Aunt Sophia and Uncle Victor, a new soccer ball and cleats, new markers and a gift certificate to Walmart, so I can buy myself whatever I want. *I'm so lucky,* I think.

"One more," Daddy says, handing me a box. "You better sit down," he says. The box shakes in his hands and almost falls before he wraps one arm around it to hold it in place before gently placing it in my lap on the floor.

My eyes wide, I raise my hand to the lid. I barely touch it when it pops up and something jumps out. Startled, I scream and push the box off my lap. A puppy squiggles around and then hops onto my lap. It's got big, flappy ears and a tan, black and white body. It yelps in my face then licks my cheek.

"Really, Daddy?" I laugh, grabbing onto the puppy as I look around for Daddy. "I get a puppy?" I ask. "Do I get to keep him?" I wrap my arm around the puppy's neck and kiss his nose.

"Of course you do." Daddy laughs, his blue eyes sparkling. "He's your birthday present from me and Mommy. Now you need to give him a name."

"Max," I say quickly. I've always wanted a puppy and already had a name picked out. "Can I show Max to Mommy?" I ask.

"She's still lying down," Daddy says. "But don't worry, she wants you to enjoy your party. This is your special day, princess. You deserve only the best things in life." He bends down and hugs me as he says this and I know it should make me feel happy, but for some reason his words make me feel sad inside. "Now go back and play with your friends, you can show Max to Mommy later."

Ariel, Cinderella and most of my friends, except for Jenny and Patricia, leave soon after my presents are opened. Aunt Sophia, Uncle Victor, Karen and Marcy go upstairs to say goodbye to Mom and then they give me a hug. I wait and play with Max as they are standing at the door talking to Daddy. They're supposed to just say a quick goodbye, but Uncle Victor and Daddy talk a lot when they see each other. Marcy and Karen have already gone out to the car. I ask Jenny and Patricia to take Max in the backyard and I sneak upstairs to check on Mommy.

"Mommy," I whisper when I get to her room. She's lying on the bed on her side facing the window. When I walk around to her, her eyes are closed and she's snoring softly. Her face is red and her eyelids are puffy, like she's been crying. She's holding a picture in her hand, so I tug on it gently to look at it. It's a picture of a little girl, maybe two or three years old. *Who is it?* I slip the picture back into her hand and give her a kiss on the cheek then go back downstairs.

Uncle Victor and Daddy have finally stopped talking and Daddy is waving at them from the doorway. Patricia and Jenny are back inside with Max. Daddy closes the door and turns to us. "You girls hungry?" he asks. We all nod. "Give me three minutes to change and I will get your dinner." He runs upstairs and within minutes he is back in front of us wearing a black suit with a white tie. "Time for dinner, princesses," he says and bows, then holds out a hand to lead us into the kitchen. "Your favourite meal awaits."

Max follows me and stays right by my feet. I watch my feet as I walk because I tripped on him a couple times already. I'm afraid I'll step on him and squish him.

I giggle. "You look like a real butler, Daddy!" Max yelps like he's agreeing with me. *I love Max already.*

The suit fits Daddy perfectly; he's tall and thin, probably because he goes running almost every day.

"I am a real butler, Princess Elaina." He bows again.

Patricia, Jenny and I laugh again and run into the kitchen, Max still on my heels. Mommy is now sitting in a corner with a blanket wrapped around her shoulders. I didn't even see her come downstairs.

"Mommy," I shout, bending down to pick up Max. He squirms in my arms and I have to hold on tight, so he doesn't wiggle right out of my hands. "Look, Mommy—my new puppy. I named him Max."

Max yelps again and he's squirming so much I have to put him down. He runs up to Mommy and jumps up, putting his front paws on her legs.

She smiles as at me, but she has a weird look on her face, like she is looking right through me and doesn't even see me. "Happy birthday, Rebecca," she says and blows me a kiss.

Rebecca?

"Sweetheart," Daddy says, rushing up to Mommy. "What are you doing out of bed? You're not feeling good, you shouldn't be down here." He puts his hands around her shoulders and helps her stand up, then leads her out of the room.

"Rebecca, Rebecca," Mommy is repeating. Her voice is getting smaller as she reaches the top of the stairs.

"Who's Rebecca?" Jenny asks.

I shrug.

"What's wrong with your mom?" Patricia asks. "Is she going crazy?"

I shrug again.

"I had an uncle that went crazy," Jenny says. "He got locked up in a nuthouse."

Patricia elbows her in the ribs. "Ow," Jenny complains. Then she looks up at me. "Oh, sorry, Laney," she says. "I didn't mean . . . um, your mom, she's not crazy. I, um, was just talking about my uncle."

"Sorry about that sweetie," Daddy says, rushing back into the kitchen and interrupting Jenny's fumbling attempt at an apology.

He holds out a chair for each of us and pushes it in to the table once we sit down. Then he picks up a tray from the counter that has three bowls of macaroni and cheese.

"Is Mommy going to get sent to a nuthouse?" I ask.

"No, no, no, don't be silly," he says. "Mommy's just not feeling good and her medicine is making her mind a little foggy. Now," he continues, placing a bowl in front of each of us, "here is your favourite meal. Royal macaroni and cheese for the royal princesses."

"Yippee!" I shout, clapping, as he sets a bowl down in front of me. We stab our forks into the macaroni and shovel it into our mouths like we're a pack of wild animals instead of fancy princesses. Max yelps at my chair and jumps up toward me. I stab some noodles onto my fork and hold it under the table so Max can have a taste. He chews on the fork until he gets off all the noodles.

"No, no, sweetie," Daddy says, coming over to me and picking Max up. "Only puppy food for Max, we can't give him people food or he'll get sick. Do you understand?"

"Yes, Daddy." I nod.

He locks Max in a dog cage and comes back with three cups of fresh strawberry juice, three bowls of fresh raspberries with whipped cream and a giant bowl of ice cream with sprinkles and little marshmallows for each of us.

I can't eat all of my ice cream, so I just eat all of the sprinkles and marshmallows and leave the rest to melt in the bowl.

I'm a real princess, I think, twirling into my bedroom after Patricia and Jenny have gone home. *This was the best birthday ever.* Max runs along behind me and crashes into my ankles when I stop. I laugh and pick him up and plunk him down on my bed. I'm so happy that Daddy said I could sleep in my princess dress tonight.

"Knock, knock," Daddy says as he opens my door. "You had a busy day—time for bed now," he says.

"Aw, come on, just five more minutes. I want to play with Max." I bend down and scratch his back. He plops over and falls onto his side, so I rub his belly. His little leg shakes and I giggle.

"Okay, but just five minutes, you understand?" he asks.

I nod and smile at him. He comes over and gives me a hug. "Happy birthday, Laney," he says, kissing me on the top of my head.

"Who's Rebecca?" I ask. I feel his body freeze for just a second then he clears his throat.

"I . . . I don't know, sweetie. Mommy just gets confused sometimes. Her medicine will help her feel better someday, I hope. But that's not for you to worry about. You need to get your teeth brushed and get to bed. Even princesses need their beauty sleep."

"Daddy, you're silly." I laugh. "I'm not a real princess."

"Of course you are! You are my real princess." He winks and bows. "Five minutes," he reminds me and leaves, pulling my bedroom door shut behind him.

I twirl over to my mirror to admire my dress again and when I see my refection, I stop dancing. I suddenly feel sick to my stomach and have to hold my breath so that I don't throw up.

As I look at my reflection, it feels wrong to have had such a good day. I don't know why, but as I look at my face in the mirror, I feel like I don't deserve to have such a good birthday. I feel like I'm living in the wrong life and I really want to know who it was I was looking for at my party earlier.

CHAPTER 3

Danica

"Get up," Benson says as he pushes my bedroom door open. "You were supposed to leave for school ten minutes ago. Stop being a lazy brat and get going."

I groan, pull the cover up over my head and roll over.

The floor creaks under his weight as he steps over to my bed. I know the sounds all too well. After his fourth step I brace myself. I'm not sure what's coming, but I know something is.

It's his foot. I feel his heel dig into my back as he shoves me. I roll into the wall, bury my face into the corner, and groan again.

"I don't feel good," I complain.

"Too bad," he says, shoving me with his foot again. "You can't keep skipping school just because you don't feel good. Suck it up and get going."

I ignore him.

I feel the blanket get yanked off me. Goosebumps erupt on my arms as the cool air hits my skin.

"I don't feel good," I say again. "Just let me stay home today. Please," I beg. I put my arms up over my head, burying my face deeper into my pillow.

"You stayed home yesterday, and the day before. That's enough. I don't want no freeloader living here. If you want to keep living under my roof, you're going to get your butt to school and not cause any trouble for us."

He grabs my shoulder and shakes me, sending a fresh wave of nausea through me.

I put a hand over my throat, trying to push the nausea back down.

"I said get going," Benson says. He grabs my arm and yanks.

My body jerks up toward him as he keeps his hand pinched around my arm and takes a step backwards, pulling me up and off my bed.

"I'm going to . . ." I heave and buck and throw up all over him. My heart stops. I rip my arm from his grip and put both hands over my mouth. "I'm sorry, I'm sorry," I mumble from beneath my hands. My eyes are wide, my unsettled stomach momentarily forgotten as I watch him, trying to read his body movements so I can prepare for the impending blow. *A slap across the face? A kick in the thigh?*

He just stares at me, his face twisting in anger as he wipes some puke from his cheek and flicks it at me. It hits me on the neck. Then he grabs my arm and pulls me again, out of my room and into the bathroom.

"Where's Crystal?" I ask, looking backwards out of the bathroom. "Crystal!" I yell. He pushes past me and closes the door then moves back to the tub. He bends over the tub and a burst of water explodes from the tap a moment later.

"Your mother is asleep," he says, without looking at me. He pulls the lever and water sprays from the shower spout. "Get in and get cleaned up," he says, pushing me toward the shower.

I stand there, watching him, waiting for him to leave.

"Hurry up," he says, not moving.

"Some privacy?" I ask, feeling my stomach start to turn again and a lump rise in my throat.

I notice my reflection in the mirror, and I'm startled by how awful I look. My eyes have dark circles underneath them and my skin is pasty and pale. My hair looks oily and ratty. I flick my tongue around in my mouth as I notice the nasty taste inside my mouth.

"You can earn your privacy when you start following the rules around here. Now get in and get to school before they call here again asking about you." He knocks the toilet lid down, sits, and adds, "And make sure you do a real good job scrubbing up."

I remain frozen, just staring at him.

He shifts, like he's going to stand up.

"Fine," I say, "whatever."

I turn around and pull my shirt over my head, letting it fall to the floor. Then I tug my pyjama bottoms. They're a little snug, so I have to tug on them again until they fall down and drop around my ankles. I step out of them quickly and into the shower. The water burns my skin and I have to adjust the knob. I pull the curtain closed behind me, but it's a clear curtain, so it doesn't offer any privacy. I keep my back to him, squeezing my eyes shut as I squirt shampoo into my hand and lather it into my hair. *Maybe I will feel better after a shower,* I decide.

As I work the shampoo into my hair, I picture myself far away, in another life, with parents who love me and take care of me. I have siblings and friends, a dog and cat, lots of food to eat and clothes that fit. I get lost in this daydream. It feels so real. I can see my house and my room. I can taste the dinner my parents set out for me. I can feel myself having fun with my friends. I'm happy, carefree, loved.

"What the fuck?" Benson shouts.

I open my eyes, startled. My back is no longer to him, I didn't notice I had turned around and I'm now facing him.

"What?" I ask when he just keeps staring at me, fury rising in his face. I have no idea what I've done to set him off, which makes his anger toward me that much scarier.

"What the fuck is wrong with your stomach?" he shouts. He's now standing and rips the shower curtain open. He's pointing at my stomach.

I look down at it. "I don't know." I shrug. "I told you I don't feel good. I think I have the flu."

He pokes me in the stomach, hard. "Ow!" I yell, pulling back and covering my stomach with my arms. It does feel hard, and it's sticking out a little. *I must be really sick,* I worry. *Or getting fat, although I don't know how—there's never much to eat in this house.*

He grabs both of my wrists and pulls my arms away from me. He's staring at my stomach; it's freaking me out. The water keeps spilling out, spraying my face.

"You didn't tell me you started getting your period," he accuses.

"I never started yet," I protest, heat rising to my face. *What business is it of his anyway?* I try to pull away from him, but he won't let go. I twist my wrists, trying to break free from his grip, but he just squeezes tighter, until I cry out in pain.

"Don't lie to me!" he shouts.

"I'm not lying," I cry. I feel a lump rise in my throat and tears escape my eyes and trickle down my cheeks, but they are quickly washed away from the shower. The nausea returns and I will it away. *He'll kill me if I barf on him again,* I think. I close my eyes and count to ten, hoping I can hold it in.

"You're pregnant!" he accuses. "You little whore," he adds, finally letting one wrist go and poking me in the stomach again.

"No, I'm not," I argue. I look down at my stomach again. *Am I?* "I'm only thirteen," I say, trying to reason with him. "I've never even had my period yet." I don't know much, but the teachers had told us a few things in health class before they gave up and cancelled the rest of the unit because the boys were too goofy and the girls too giggly. "Don't you have to have a period in order to get pregnant?"

"Who's the little shit who knocked you up?" he shouts. "Does your mother know you have a boyfriend? What kind of girl is she raising?" He's ranting now. Spit bubbles are starting to pool in the corners of his mouth, and some are flying out and hitting me in the face as he yells.

"I don't have a boyfriend," I say, starting to shiver. The water has turned cold and is now beating down on me with an icy spray.

"Didn't your mother ever talk to you about boys?" he asks. "What the hell are you doing with them?"

"Nothing! There are no boys!" I yell back this time. I'm afraid. He's never looked so crazy before. It's like he's possessed.

I step out of the shower and grab for a towel that's hanging on the rack to try to cover up. It's only a hand towel so it doesn't do much. I move to step around him and he moves with me, blocking my escape.

"You're pregnant," he spits, putting his hand across the hard lump in my belly.

No. I can't be.

"Does your mother know about this? Did she let this happen?"

The room is spinning. I reach out and grab onto the counter in order to keep from passing out. I let the towel fall and cover my belly with my free hand. *Is there a little lump?*

"Tell me who the father is," he says, grabbing my chin and pinching as he pulls my face toward his. "Tell me," he repeats.

I don't know what's going on. *How can he ask me this?* I'm so confused. The room continues to spin.

"Who did this to you?" he asks again. He's grunting and spitting as he breathes; his spit already tastes of beer despite the early hour. I gag and cover my mouth.

He pinches my chin harder. "Answer me," he says.

I look straight into his eyes, stand up straight and step toward him. "You," I say. "You did this to me. Or one of your stupid friends."

Whack.

My head whips to the side as his open hand connects with my cheek. I see my reflection, in slow motion, in the mirror, my lips moving side to side as my face swings away from his slap.

"Don't you even try to pin this on me, you lying little brat," he spits again.

"It is you," I say again, feeling stronger now that the words are out. "You're the one who comes into my room at night, after Crystal falls asleep. You're the one who . . ."

Whack.

He's punched me in the stomach. I bend over, grabbing my belly. I can't breathe. A pain shoots through my stomach and across my back.

He grabs a handful of my hair and pulls, lifting my face up to his. I'm trying to catch my breath, to get some oxygen into my lungs.

"Don't you ever say that again," he says, squeezing his fist tighter, pulling my hair from the roots. "Or you'll be sorry," he threatens.

I'm already sorry, I think.

With his free hand he punches me in the stomach again, harder this time.

"Ow!" I cry out. "Stop!" Tears are falling freely down my face.

I move my arms in front of my stomach, blocking his next blow. His fist connects with my forearm and I cry out again. It feels like my bones have cracked. Then he balls my hand up into a fist, covers it with his own, and forces me to punch myself repeatedly in the stomach.

I can't fight anymore; my arms go limp as he punches me again and again with my own fist. I feel snot dripping from my nose and taste it as it falls into my mouth.

"Crystal!" I yell. "Mom, I need you," I say over and over, but my voice is barely above a whisper. I have no fight left in me. I have no voice to call for help. I am at the mercy of a mad man.

Finally, Benson lets me go. I fall to the ground and curl up, my body shaking and heaving as I try to catch my breath.

His bare feet are inches away from my face, so I squeeze my eyes shut and start rocking myself. My body bucks and slides across the floor as he gives one last kick to my stomach. It's hard enough to push me back into the bathtub. I scream out as the pain shoots through me, down my legs, through my arms. My stomach feels like it has been turned inside out. My head feels like it's going to explode. I can feel a wetness between my legs and when I open my eyes to look, I see that it's blood.

I close my eyes again when I see him bending toward me. He brushes my hair back softly, away from my ear and I cringe when I feel his lips against my ear. "Remember," he whispers, "I can go get your sister to replace you anytime I want." I can feel his evil smile through his words, and it sends a new chill through me. He drapes his fingers slowly from my head, down my side and all along the side of my leg. At my ankle he pinches some skin up between his fingers and twists. I don't even feel it above the pain that is already surging through my body.

He stands, turns and walks out of the bathroom, pulling the door shut behind him.

I watch him disappear behind the closed door and am thankful that he is gone. My arm is twitching uncontrollably. My entire body hurts. I can't take the pain anymore. It's too much. I can't bear it. So, I do the only thing I can—I use the only weapon I have to protect myself. I leave my body and the pain completely behind. I think about that other girl, in the other life, full of happiness and joy. I think about her until I can't feel anything at all. I see myself, lying broken and bleeding on the floor, but I am no longer in there. I am no longer suffering.

It's the weirdest feeling to be able to see myself, to know that I am hurting, but to not feel any sensations of pain at all. It's the only way I've learned to survive. It's the only way I know to feel free. I close my eyes and bask in the feeling of nothingness.

"Danny, Danny, are you okay?"

I feel my body move as someone's shaking me. I open my eyes, but I can't see, the light's too bright.

"It's me, it's Mom," Crystal says. "Daddy said you needed me, that you got your period," she says.

"What? No," I say.

My eyes finally focus, and I see Benson standing in the doorway. His arms are crossed and he's staring at me like he wants to kill me, like he's wishing he had killed me.

"Well, it sure looks like you did," Crystal says, nodding toward my bottom half with her chin.

I look down and the bath mat I'm lying on is covered in blood.

"Go away, honey," Crystal says, getting up and closing the door. "We have girl business to attend to in here." The door clicks and he's gone. "Now," she says, turning back to me, "this is nothing to freak out about." She staggers a little as she walks back toward me and grabs the sink for support. Her hair is pulled back as usual, with wild strands around her face. Her mascara has smudged so that she has big black circles around both eyes.

She reaches down and puts her hands under my armpits, trying to pull me up. I stay limp at first to make it harder for her, but she just keeps pulling on me, scraping my skin with her dry hands. She's breathing her nasty breath into my face, a combination of vodka, cigarettes and morning breath.

I turn my face away from her.

"It's nothing to be embarrassed about," she says, misreading the reason for me turning my face away.

She lifts the toilet lid with her foot and sits me down on it. "You could have taken care of this yourself," she scolds. "I told you where the pads are."

My hands are still cradling my stomach. I feel a new wave of pain shoot through me. I want to go away again, to leave the pain, but she won't let me. She keeps talking to me, keeping me here with her.

She reaches under the sink and pulls out a pad. "Now, you know what to do with this, right?"

I nod and bend over, wrapping my arms tighter around my stomach, which is cramping and twisting. I moan.

"It really hurts," I complain.

"You're going to get cramps," she says. "Just rub your belly and you'll be fine. You're a big girl now," she says, rubbing my back, "so that means you're going to have to start taking care of yourself. So, get in that shower and clean up. Then clean up this floor, it's gross. I'd help you but you know how I feel about blood." She shudders in disgust as she looks around the bathroom. "And don't you have to be in school? What day is it today?" She looks out the window, confused, as if she's surprised she can't tell what day it is by what the weather is doing outside.

"I can't," I protest.

"You can and you will, missy," she says, waving a finger at me. "You can't go missing school just because you got your period. Now get going."

I stay put, squeezing my arms against my belly and moan loudly again.

"All right, all right," she says, "you don't need to be a big baby about it. We all go through it. Here"—she reaches into the cabinet above the sink and pulls out a little container of aspirin—"take two of these. You better get used to it." She's looking at me but her eyes are blurry and unfocused. She kisses me on the top of the head and disappears out of the bathroom, pulling the door closed behind her.

I bury my hands in my face and cry, rocking back and forth on the toilet until the cramping finally slows down, until the pain has gone for real. I rub my eyes, which I can feel are swollen and puffy, and look around the bathroom. It looks like someone was massacred in here. There is blood all over the floor, and bloody footprints, both hers and Benson's, lead to the door.

I reach for the pill bottle and consider swallowing the entire bottle of aspirin, but when I open it up, I see there are only five pills inside, and I'm pretty sure that won't do anything. I duck my face under the tap and take in a gulp of water then pop two pills and put the container back in the cabinet. I grab the hand towel, wet it and start mopping up the blood. I rinse and wipe, rinse and wipe, until all that's left is a faint pink stain on the floor.

I fold the bath mat up and stuff it into the garbage bin then I step inside the tub, pulling the useless see-through curtain closed behind me and turn the water on again. I scrub my face, digging my fists into my eyes, determined to wash away all evidence of tears. My body hurts with every move, but I scrub the dried blood from my body, turning my skin pink from the heat and the scrubbing. I watch the red water swirl at my feet and disappear down the drain and wish that the drain would open up and swallow me whole.

Back in my room, I dress quickly, pulling on a pair of jogging pants and an old T-shirt. I brush the knots out of my hair and grab my backpack. I move quickly down the stairs, taking them two at a time.

"Want Benson to drive you to school when he gets back from the store?" Crystal asks. "He'll be back in a couple minutes." She's back on the couch, feet up, back propped against a pillow. She has a blanket pulled up around her chin. Her eyes are dopey, and she looks past me instead of at me as she talks.

There's an open pill bottle that's not aspirin, and a half-empty bottle of beer on the coffee table beside her.

"No, I'll walk," I say, stepping into my shoes and running out the door. I need to get out before Benson gets back.

A car squeals and pulls into our driveway just after I step outside. I have to jump out of the way so I don't get hit.

Benson slams on the brakes and the car jerks to a stop. He gets out, slams the door and holds out his hand to me.

"Here," he says, pushing a little container into my hand. "Keep your mouth shut and take one of these every day. Don't you miss any, you hear me? I'll get you more when you need them."

I open my palm and see a container with little pills arranged into a circle.

"Where'd you get these?" I ask.

"Doesn't matter," he snarls, "just take them and shut up. And don't you ever get yourself knocked up again. You got it?"

I nod and he turns away, leaving me standing in the driveway with a container of pills.

I look down at them and wonder if there is any chance that swallowing this entire container of pills at once could kill me.

My lips curl up into a smile at the thought.

CHAPTER 4

Elaina

"Night night, Elly Belly," a little girl says. She looks exactly like me.

She lifts my pyjama top, puts her face on my belly and blows. I squeal and try to push her face away. I'm laughing so hard that I can't move her. She does another raspberry on my belly, making me laugh some more. I force myself to take a big breath and I squirm and giggle and wiggle around in my bed.

She finally stops and pulls the blanket up over me. She tucks it under my arms and grabs a raggedy old stuffed rabbit and tucks it into the crook of my elbow. "Hold on tight to Bunny Boo," she says. "Now, you remember what I told you, right?" she asks. She's serious now, no more laughing. The light from the window is shining onto her face.

I nod.

"It's very important," she says. "Are you sure you remember everything?"

I nod again.

"What did I tell you?"

"Be quiet," I say, smiling. I'm proud that I remembered.

"It's more than that," she says. She looks mad. I don't like when she looks like that.

"Be invisible," she says.

"Like a ghost?" I ask. I remember the cartoons I saw with ghosts in them.

"Exactly," she says.

"Are ghosts real?" I ask. I feel my heartbeat quicken. I'm afraid of ghosts.

"No," she assures me. I believe her because I know she'd never lie to me.

"But monsters are real," I say.

"Yes, monsters are real," she answers.

"I'm scared of monsters," I say. My lower lip comes up in a pout.

"Don't be scared," she says. "I'll never let any monsters hurt you, Elly Belly." She tickles my belly from above the blanket and we both laugh. "You just have to remember to do exactly what I say, okay?"

I nod again. I will do whatever she tells me to.

"So close your eyes and go right to sleep," she says.

"I will."

"And don't make any noise. No matter what. You understand?"

"Yes."

"Even if you wake up in the middle of the night."

"Okay. Wait, what if I need to pee?"

"You have to hold it 'til morning. You can do it."

"Okay."

"And if you have a bad dream, just squeeze Bunny Boo—he'll make you feel better. But remember, do not move, okay?"

"Okay." I give Bunny Boo a squeeze, just to make sure he's in the right spot.

"And if you hear any monsters come in the room, just bury your head in your pillow, keep your eyes closed and sing your song in your head. Over and over. Keep singing until you fall back to sleep. But don't sing out loud, only sing in your head. You understand?"

"Yes," I say.

"It's important that you do exactly what I say." She looks angry again.

"I know. I'll do what you say."

"Good. Night night, Elly Belly," she says. "I love you. I'll always protect you." She kisses me on the cheek and disappears, shaking the bed and making it creak.

I watch the lights from our window as they make shadows against the wall until I get tired and fall asleep.

Sometime later I hear a click and I wake up right away. *The monster is coming.*

I squeeze Bunny Boo. His ear is touching my face, so I turn my head an inch and kiss his ear, just so he's not scared.

Light comes in the room from the hallway when the monster opens the door.

I hold my breath and count his footsteps as he walks toward the bed. When the footsteps stop, the bed shakes and creaks.

I squeeze my eyes shut and bury my head in my pillow. In my head I start singing the song she taught me. *Go away, monster, I'm not afraid of you. I'll make you go away, I know what to do. I keep my eyes closed and sing my song. And when I wake up, you'll be gone.*

I sing the song over and over in my head as the monster moves around and shakes the bed.

I sing the song again, then stop and listen.

The monster is still here. The song's not working.

I'm scared. I don't know what to do. The girl—I think she's my sister—she taught me this song to chase the monster away. *My sister! She's down there with the monster. I have to help her.*

I sing the song again. Really loud. I yell the words in my head. *I need to chase the monster away before he hurts her.*

I hold my breath and listen. The monster is still here.

I have to help her.

The monster is hurting her.

I hug Bunny Boo again and count to three, trying to get some courage.

One.

Two.

Three.

I have to do something before I chicken out.

I throw Bunny Boo across the room. His face hits the window and his button eyes make a loud cracking sound against the glass. "Don't hurt Annie!" I scream. "Don't hurt Annie. Don't hurt Annie." I repeat the same words over and over as loud as I can. I need to save her from the monster. "Don't hurt Annie!" My throat is burning because I'm screaming so loud.

Suddenly, I'm awake. I jump up and out of bed. Max follows me off the bed and he's circling around my legs, whining. I put my hand up to my throat; it's sore. I look around and realize I'm alone in my room. A little table lamp shines from the corner, the way it does every single night while I sleep. There's no monster. There's no Annie. *Who is Annie?*

"Elaina, honey, are you okay?" My door shoots open and my dad is running toward me.

He's panting. He must have run from his bedroom when he heard me.

"You were screaming," he says. "Are you okay?" He comes over and hugs me. Wrapped up in his arms, I feel safe again.

"I just had a bad dream, that's all it was." My body trembles as relief washes over me. "It was just a dream," I say. "It was just a dream," I repeat, trying to convince him.

But it doesn't feel like a dream.

It feels like a memory.

I spend the rest of the night tossing and turning. I don't have any more nightmares, but I don't get much more sleep either. I'm trying to force myself to remember. Remember what? I'm not sure, but I feel like there is something I'm forgetting.

I must finally have fallen back to sleep because I'm startled awake when I hear a knock at my door. My clock says 6:38. I look out my window and it's surprisingly light out considering the time. *Snow day?*

"You awake?" Dad asks with another knock on my door.

"Come in," I say as I roll out of bed and walk over to my window. There's at least two feet of new snow on the roof of the house behind us and it's still coming down in big, fat flakes.

"Buses are cancelled today," Dad says.

"Yes," I say, raising my arms in triumph. "Hey, wait. Why'd you wake me up then?" I ask, irritated.

"I was going to leave for work, but I can wait and drive you to school first if you go get ready."

"It's a snow day," I complain. "I don't want to go to school on a snow day."

"School is important," he argues.

"No one's even going to be there," I argue back. "Snow day equals day off, Dad. Everyone knows that. I don't want to be the only loser stuck in school when everyone else gets to stay home."

"If everyone else jumped off a bridge, would you jump off a bridge, too?" he asks. It's his stupid go-to question whenever he wants to remind me to have my own mind and not be a follower.

"I would if it got me a day off school," I say, smirking. I'm tired and cranky this morning and not in the mood for his stupid parental lessons.

"Mom's not having a good morning," he cautions, "I don't want you to stay home alone with her."

"See, then she needs me at home today to help take care of her. So, you go to work and I'll stay home with her. Good talk, good talk," I say and climb back into bed. I pull the blanket up over my head. I'm so tired all I want to do is fall back to sleep.

"You're cranky today," he says.

"I didn't sleep much."

"More nightmares?"

"Just the one," I say and flip my blanket off my face, "but it took forever to fall back to sleep."

"You haven't had many nightmares lately," he comments.

"No," I say. "Is that unusual?" I ask.

"You don't remember?" he asks.

I shake my head and sit up. *What's he talking about?*

"You used to have a lot of nightmares when you were little."

"I did?"

"I'm surprised you don't remember them. You had one almost every night for a long time. Your doctor said it was night terrors and that you'd eventually outgrow them. You haven't had one in so long I thought you had. Was this one about monsters, too?"

I twist my head quickly to look at him. *How did he know?*

"Did you sing your song to chase them away?" he asks.

"What song?" I ask quickly. I'm instantly awake and I feel my heart racing. "What song?" I ask again when he doesn't answer.

"You used to sing a song whenever you had a bad dream. You said it chased the monsters away. How did it go?" He raises his hand and holds his chin between his thumb and forefinger and rests his elbow on his knee as he thinks. "Go away, monster . . ."

Oh my God, the song is real.

"You don't scare me," he says. "No wait, that's not right." He's squinting now and his face is scrunched up, like he's trying really hard to think.

My heart is pumping so hard I can feel the blood being forced through my veins. My head feels dizzy, like the blood is rushing to my brain too fast.

"Go away, monster, I'm not afraid of you. I'll make you go away, I know what to do. I keep my eyes closed and sing my song. And when I wake up, you'll be gone." I sing the song slowly as he watches me.

"Yes." He smiles and snaps his fingers. "That's it. That's the song."

He looks thrilled that I remembered it, but I feel like I could throw up. My head feels cool and sweaty and I start to tremble. *Who taught me that song?*

I stand at the window and watch Dad's car disappear down the road. Max, as usual, is at my feet, leaning against me. I scratch his head. It had taken a lot of begging and pleading and some fake tears, but Dad had finally agreed to let me stay home. He made me promise to leave Mom alone and not bother her. I told him I would probably just sleep half the day anyway.

But now that he's gone, I need to find some answers. I don't know what I'm looking for, so I decide to just start digging through everything.

Four hours later, I have nothing. Max had given up on following me around after the first hour and had climbed up on the couch for a nap. I had gone through the entire house except Mom and Dad's room because Mom was sleeping in there and the basement storage room because it was dark and creepy and full of cobwebs. All that I had learned was that we are a boring family.

Disappointed, I quickly make a peanut butter and jam sandwich to stop my stomach from rumbling and sink into the couch to eat it. I'm sweating from pulling things out of cupboards and closets and putting everything back exactly as I had found it.

I close my eyes to think as I pop the last corner of sandwich into my mouth. I almost fall asleep as I'm chewing so decide to give up. *This is a waste of time,* I think. I decide the rest of my day would be better spent in bed, so I open my eyes and stand up.

I notice a framed picture of me from my eighth birthday party on one of the bookcase shelves. I'm dolled up like a princess. I smile when I remember how much fun I had and Dad following me around with his camera. I realize that I've never looked at any of the pictures he took that day, so I pull out the photo albums. There are only three of them squeezed in between other books on a very full shelf.

There must be more albums somewhere because these ones are random. The first one is only half full and has pictures from the past few months. The second one has pictures from the year I was ten, the one and only summer I played baseball. The last one has pictures of me when I was little, maybe five or six. In some of the pictures I'm smiling, but in others I look sad, or even scared. *Was it the night terrors?* I wonder.

I flip to the back of the album and a picture falls out and lands face-down on the floor. I turn it over and see it's a picture of a little girl. I recognize the picture; I've seen it once before. I hold it beside one of my pictures and compare them.

It's definitely not me.

Who is it?

CHAPTER 5

Danica

"Give me that," I say, grabbing the bottle of vodka from Brent. He grunts in complaint as I pull the bottle from his lips. The clear liquid dribbles down his chin and he wipes it away with his sleeve after he lets go of the bottle. I tilt my head back and take a big gulp. It burns my throat and immediately heats my insides. I almost spit it out, but instead I force it down with another gulp. After the fourth sip I start to like the burn that is radiating throughout my body.

"My turn now," Matt says, grabbing it from my mouth, knocking the lip of the bottle off my front teeth.

"Ow, watch it," I say, rubbing my teeth to make sure he didn't chip them.

"Don't be a baby," Brent says, grabbing the bottle from Matt.

"Hey," he complains, lifting the bottle to look at the little bit of liquid sloshing around at the bottom, "it's almost gone." He takes a quick drink and makes a funny noise as he swallows it down.

"Let me have the rest?" I ask, reaching for the bottle.

"No way," Brent says, swinging the bottle out of my reach. "I hardly had any." I take another step toward the moving bottle and trip, stumbling into him.

I giggle as I hold on to Brent until I regain my balance. Brent and Matt laugh with me.

"Come on, please?" I beg. I tilt my head, push out my lower lip and bat my eyelashes at them.

"No way," he repeats, "I'm the one who's going to get killed if my dad realizes I stole it from his liquor cabinet. So that means I get to finish it."

"Come on," I argue, "you can always get another bottle."

"Not a chance," Brent says. "He keeps his liquor cabinet locked. I got lucky this morning, it's the first time he's ever forgotten to lock it. I know, I've checked a hundred times."

"Shhh, someone's coming," I say, still giggling as a car pulls up into the parking lot and a man and woman get out. They look like they're a couple, probably someone's parents here for a parent/teacher interview. *Good thing it's not Crystal and Benson*, I think, but then remember that they've never been to one parent/teacher interview that I can remember.

Brent holds the bottle behind his back, and we stare at them, doing our best to stand still and not giggle as they walk past us. They look at us, three nerdy teenagers standing beside a dumpster in the parking lot behind the school, trying to look sober. They pretend they don't see us then they disappear into the school.

"Don't be such a drama queen," I say, punching Brent in the arm when the door shuts behind the couple. "Please?" I ask again. The sun is shining brightly, so I have to squint when I look at him.

"What do I get for it?" he asks, smiling wickedly at me.

I look around, checking to see if there is anyone else walking around. It's the first sunny day after a long, cold winter, which should mean that there will be a lot more kids skipping class like us today. If they are, they've found somewhere better to go. The three of us are all alone. It probably has something to do with the fact that we're standing beside a dumpster, which you can usually smell from twenty feet away. It must have just been emptied, though, as there is no smell today. Either that or the vodka fumes are masking the smell.

"My undying gratitude and appreciation," I offer. I smile and raise my eyebrows at him.

I look at them, scrawny boys with greasy hair and zit-covered faces. Brent has dark hair that he usually wears short, but he's started growing it recently to piss off his mother. It curls up at the base of his neck and he has started an annoying habit of constantly swinging his head to the side to get his bangs out of his eyes. He wore his usual baggy jeans and dark hoodie. Matt, on the other hand, has always worn his hair long. It hangs down in his face, covering most of his eyes and nose. He has a piercing in his eyebrow, one in his lip and six in his left ear. He dresses the opposite of Brent, with his skin-tight jeans and tight flannel shirt, usually in some sort of crazy colour like the pink-and-yellow one he's wearing today, which he always buttons up right to the top.

I've known each of them since the first day of high school when we met in the cafeteria. We all ended up at the same table because we had no one else to sit with. We just kind of clicked and we've hung out at school every day since. Matt and Brent hung around outside of school as well and for the first year of high school they invited me to hang out with them. After a year of me turning them down they stopped asking. I love hanging out with them, and they're the best friends that I have, but it's just easier for me to keep it limited to an at-school friendship. Benson always tracks my whereabouts and I'm sure he'd have an issue with me hanging out with not one, but two guys. Plus, I would never bring a friend home, male or female, to the personal hellhole which I am forced to call home.

I look at the bottle; there's still at least an inch of vodka left, and I really like the way it is making me feel. "Pretty please," I beg again, nodding toward the bottle.

"Oh fine," Brent grumbles and shoves the bottle into my hand. I gulp it down, enjoying the burning pain that shoots down my throat. I still don't like the taste, but I like the effects that are starting to take shape.

I shake my head, hoping to spread the fog that's invading my mind.

The school bell rings, signalling the end of another boring school day. I throw the empty bottle up into the dumpster and we hear it smash and break on the bottom. "Awesome!" Brent says, and he and Matt high-five each other.

We start walking through the parking lot that is now full with students pouring out of the school. Some have already reached their cars and whiz past us, honking and swerving like maniacs.

"Wait," I say, grabbing Brent's arm when I see my math teacher push through the door. "Mr. Jans." I signal, pointing with my chin. I step behind Brent. "Hide me," I say. "He'll totally rat me out if he sees me. I'm already going to fail his class."

Brent and Matt stop and stand shoulder to shoulder. I have my head lowered and tucked against Brent's back. For some reason, I've always felt very safe with Brent around.

"He's gone," Matt says.

"Cool, thanks," I say, pushing between them. I link one arm in each of theirs and we continue walking through the parking lot. I wish I could keep walking like this with them to protect me straight into a new life and a new family.

"Want us to walk you home?" Brent asks when we reach the edge of the school property.

"No, I'm good," I say. "But thanks. I'll see you guys tomorrow."

"Later," they say together. I turn and wiggle my hips as I walk, sure that I have their full attention as I disappear down the sidewalk.

"Your school called," Benson says when I walk in the door and drop my school bag in front of the closet. My heart immediately starts racing, but I feel brave. Instead of looking away as I usually do, I stare right at him.

"So?" I say. I kick off my shoes and fling them across the room, knowing that it irritates him when shoes are scattered all over the front hall.

"The secretary said you missed your math class today," he says as he watches my shoes land, one propped up against a side table and the other tipped over in the middle of the hallway. "That it's the fifth time you've missed that class this month," he continues, not commenting on my shoes, although I can see his mouth tense as he keeps staring at them. "She asked if everything was okay. She asked if you wanted an appointment with the school nurse," he says, returning his attention to me.

"So?" I repeat. I grab a cigarette from the coffee table, light it, and blow the smoke toward him. The room spins from the vodka and I grab on to the door to steady myself.

"You little shit," he says, grabbing the cigarette from my hand. "We don't need this kind of attention. Go to school and stop being a little brat."

"You're not my dad. You can't tell me what to do," I say. I've never spoken back to Benson like this before. It must be the vodka. I feel invincible. For the first time in my life I'm not afraid of him.

"Want to bet?" he says, grabbing my wrist and pulling it toward him. I flinch in pain as he squeezes and turns my wrist over. Then he takes the cigarette from my fingers and puts it out in my soft flesh, right on the inside of my elbow.

"Ow! You jerk!" I yell, trying to pull my arm back, but he keeps his hold on it, pressing the cigarette deeper into my skin. "Crystal," I yell. "Mom, where are you?" I yell louder as I buckle under the piercing pain in my arm.

"She's not here." He smirks. His eyes have darkened, and he looks like a demon coming to life, garnering strength from my pain.

"Where is she?" I ask, surprised. "She never goes out." I pull away from him, although he keeps his hand gripped around my wrist and I look around the living room. The couch is empty. I don't remember the last time I saw her any place other than the couch, in various stages of inebriation or on her way into a drug- or alcohol-induced coma.

"None of your business," he says. "And stop smoking these things," he says, flicking the crushed cigarette butt away. "They're making you look old and haggard, like your mother. My profits are already down. You're not as cute as you used to be, you know."

"Like I care," I spit at him. *I love vodka!*

He leans in toward me, stopping when his face is just inches from mine. His breath is hot and musty, making my gag reflex kick in. I hold my breath and cover my nose with my free hand. "Maybe it's time I go find that sister of yours," he snarls, wiping my spit from his face. "I could use some fresh meat around here. I'm getting sick of your shit anyway," he says.

I'm instantly sober. My stomach twists, and I'm frozen in fear. *Elly.*

"Ha ha," he laughs. "Maybe you do care after all, huh?"

"You don't even know where she is," I challenge.

"Of course I do," he says, "and I can get her anytime I want."

I look away and don't say anything. My heart is pounding so hard I can see my pulse thump in my wrist under his grip.

"What's my name?" he asks.

"Benson," I say, staring at him.

He squeezes my arm again, hard. I force back a scream, not wanting to give him the satisfaction of knowing he's hurting me. "What's my name?" he repeats. "Or shall I ask your sister?" he adds when I don't answer.

I stare at him for a moment, trying to figure out if he's bluffing. When he leans over and reaches for his car keys, I decide he's telling the truth and I can't risk it. "Daddy," I say.

"That's better," he says.

Vodka has its limits. It might make me feel invincible, but that won't help Elly if he goes looking for her.

"Now go up to your room," he says. "I got a couple friends coming over tonight."

As I walk away, I consider my options. *Who am I kidding? I have no options.*

I get up and go to my room, stopping at the fridge and grabbing three beers, which I tuck under my shirt before running up the stairs.

I drink the first beer slowly, gagging after each sip; it tastes disgusting. As I watch the minutes on my clock pass by, I feel the familiar fog from the vodka start to return. By the time I'm done the first beer I feel pretty good. I drink the second one a little faster and my room starts to spin. By the time I'm halfway through the third I feel like I'm flying through the sky, or out on a rocky boat in the middle of the ocean. Either way, I'm feeling good. I chug the last half of the bottle quickly and toss it aside before I topple face-down onto my bed.

When I wake up the next morning, I'm sore everywhere. There are teeth marks on my shoulder, and I have a new cigarette burn on my other arm to match the one Benson gave me. I have a bruise in the shape of a handprint on my thigh. I feel vomit rise in my throat, but I force it back down.

My door swings open and Benson comes in. "School today, remember?" he says as I fumble to try to cover myself with the blanket.

Jerk.

"We don't want anyone to start asking questions now, do we?" he asks. He turns to leave then stops. "By the way," he says, "good work last night. Whatever you did, keep it up. Rocco and Les both paid double the usual price. And it wasn't even your birthday." He winks at me and closes the door behind him.

I try hard to remember, but all I feel is the fogginess from the alcohol. I can't remember a single thing after finishing the third beer and tossing it aside. My room does a flip-flop around me and

I roll out of bed, kneel over my little garbage container and throw up into it. I hold my face in the bucket, waiting for the next wave of puke to hit.

I can't remember a single thing! I think happily.

CHAPTER 6

Elaina

"Welcome, Elaina," the woman says. "Please have a seat," she continues, gesturing to a couch. She takes a seat in a burgundy chair with big cushions across from the couch.

"It's Laney," I say.

"Laney," she repeats, "I'm Dr. Grenner. It's a pleasure to meet you." She smiles and holds out her hand. I shake it quickly; her palm is soft and warm. Her green eyes are bright and seem to be smiling, too. They remind me of my mother's eyes, the way they used to be, before she was sick. Now she's confused all the time. She never looks at me, but is always looking around me, or through me. It's creepy.

"Am I supposed to lie down?" I ask, looking at the matching burgundy couch. It looks so comfortable and I am tired. I think about lying down and having a nap. "That's what crazy people do, right? Lie on a couch while someone tries to shrink them?"

"First of all," she says, "you're not crazy. Secondly," she continues, "I'm not going to shrink you. We're just going to talk. Sit down, lie down, do whatever you're comfortable with."

I want to dislike her, but her voice is soft and soothing, and I feel like it's putting me into a trance. She's wearing a plum-coloured pantsuit and pointy black heels. I wonder briefly how she could walk in such high heels.

I remember she's watching me, and I decide to sit, because, as she said, I'm not crazy.

"Please"—she pauses—"tell me why you are here today."

I look around her office. Two big bookcases filled with boring-looking books sit in one corner. There's a huge plant with green and yellow leaves in another corner. She has a big burgundy desk, the same colour as the couches, and I briefly wonder why everything is a shade of purple. The top of the desk is empty except for a little plant in the centre. There are two big windows and the sun shines brightly through them. I can see a forest through the windows; the leaves have started turning and there is a sea of reds, oranges and yellows.

I wish I could be out in that forest, a tiny speck, lost with the beauty of the gigantic forest instead of sitting on this couch, a single ant under her magnifying glass.

"My dad made me come," I say. I chew on a fingernail, getting a grip on a piece and ripping it off. I flinch in pain and wrap my finger in the cuff of my sweater to stop the blood that has escaped through the broken skin.

"Why did your dad want you to come?"

I shrug.

She looks down into the clipboard she's holding on her lap. Her blond hair falls in front of her face as she reads.

"How old are you?" she asks.

"Fourteen."

"Tell me about your parents," she says.

"They're okay," I answer.

"Just okay?" she asks.

"My dad's great. Mom was great, too, but she's sick now. She has Alzheimer's or something. She calls me Rebecca sometimes, but it's no big deal."

"How does that make you feel?"

"It used to bother me. But Dad says she's sick, she can't help it, so whatever." I shrug.

"And your friends? Tell me about them."

"I have a lot of friends. Jenny and Patty are my best friends, though. We hang out a lot and play soccer together. We call ourselves TY."

"Why is that?"

"Triple Y, because our names all end in a 'Y', at least our nicknames do. I don't know," I look away, embarrassed. "It sounded cool when we were kids and it just stuck. I guess it's kind of lame."

"It's not lame," she argues, "it's fun to feel a connection like that with your friends. Something that locks you together, seals your friendship in a way."

"I guess."

"I see you have a broken leg," she says, pointing to a cast on my right leg.

I don't say anything.

"Did you get that when you got in a fight with Jenny?" she asks.

I don't answer.

"Do you and Jenny fight often?" she asks.

I stay silent, looking down at my cast.

I expect her to keep speaking, but she doesn't. I can feel her looking at me and I force myself to keep my eyes facing down. I stare at my cast and feel ashamed as I remember how it happened.

Eventually, the silence gets so awkward that I look up. She's staring right at me, like she's willing me to speak.

So, I do.

"It's no big deal," I start.

I look at her again, hoping this is enough.

She continues to watch me with her big, doe-eyed stare.

"Patty and I were sleeping at Jenny's house. I had a bad dream, fell off the bed and broke my ankle. Like I said, no big deal."

"You broke your ankle falling out of bed?" she questions.

"I was on the top bunk."

"Go on," she prods, staring at me again. It's like she has truth serum in her eyes and as much as I don't want to be here, as much as I don't want to talk, words keep escaping my lips.

"We stayed up late watching a scary movie—it must have freaked me out. Jenny got a new bed, bunk beds, and we were excited to have our first sleepover in it. I slept in the top bunk and Jenny and Patty slept on the bottom, because it's a double and the top is only a single and I won the coin flip. I must have had a nightmare because of the movie. I got freaked out, jumped out of bed and hurt my ankle."

"Do you have a lot of nightmares?"

I shrug.

"Do you have a lot of nightmares?" she repeats.

"Sometimes."

"Have you always had them?"

"My dad said I did when I was a little girl. I used to sing a song to make them go away. Then they stopped for a long time and I forgot about them. I've been having nightmares again the past year or two, just once in a while. They're weird, though," I say, meeting her eyes. I decide to stop; I've said too much.

"What do you mean they're weird?" she asks.

I can't tell her. She'll definitely tell me it's time to lie down.

"The song, do you still sing it to make the nightmares go away?" she asks when I don't answer.

I shake my head.

"Why not?"

"The song's not for the nightmares," I say.

"What is it for?"

I look away, focus on my foot that is not covered in a cast, which is bouncing up and down on the floor like I'm jacked up on caffeine.

"What's the song for, Laney?" she asks.

"It's for the monster," I whisper.

"The monster?"

I look at her and nod my head slightly. *I'll be joining Jenny's uncle in no time.*

"What did you mean when you said your dreams were weird?" she asks.

Damn, she's like a dog with a bone. Why can't she just drop it already?

"What's weird about them?"

"They're not nightmares, really. I think they're memories," I confess. "Should I lie down now?" I laugh.

She smiles. "You're not crazy, Laney. It is possible that you have some repressed memories that are coming back to you in your sleep. It could be your subconscious working its way through problems you've buried deep inside your memory."

"What problems could I have buried? I have a great life," I say. "Argh," I grunt and hit my thigh with a fist. "This is so frustrating. I have absolutely nothing to complain about. Other than a sick mother, my life is perfect. What if—" I suddenly think of an idea but stop speaking when I realize it makes me sound even crazier than I already do.

"Go on," she says.

"Never mind," I say, "it's stupid."

"Nothing's stupid. I want to hear what you were going to say."

Why do I keep talking even though I don't want to? It's like she's taken away my free will. "What if they're memories from a past life? Maybe I just need to go see a psychic or something. No offense to you," I say, "because, I know, ah, what you do is really important, too." *Now I'm babbling like a fool.*

"Well," she says, "do you really think that's what's happening?"

"I guess not," I finally say, lowering my head shamefully like I'm a child who's just been scolded. *Although that would be a lot cooler than the alternative.*

She looks down at her notes again. "What happened to Jenny?"

I look up, afraid.

"You're not in trouble, Laney. I just want to know how Jenny got hurt," she says.

"I scratched her," I whisper.

"Why?"

I shrug.

"You thought she was hurting Patty?" she prods.

I nod.

"Why did you think that?"

"I—I don't know. I must have been having a nightmare. I heard the bed creak and I looked down and saw someone climbing into the bottom bunk." I look at my hands; my fingers are purple, I'm squeezing them together so tight. I feel like I'm back on the bunk bed. My heart races, my eyes are wide open, but all I see is darkness and a monster moving across the room. I can't move; I'm frozen in fear. I have to pretend I'm sleeping, or the monster will hurt me, too. I start singing my song, but I can't make it go away this time. The monster climbs onto the bottom bunk and the whole bed moves, the bed creaks and without thinking I leap over the railing, slamming my fists against its back, knocking it down as my feet hit the floor. I hear my ankle crack, but I don't feel any pain. I keep punching and scratching, trying to knock the monster away.

"Don't hurt Annie!" I scream, my fists flailing. I jump up off the couch and Dr. Grenner flinches. Startled, I look around the room and remember where I am. I remember my cast and lift my foot to take the weight off of it, waver a little, and have to grab the back of the couch to keep me from falling over.

"Who's Annie?" she asks.

I look up, confused.

"You just said, 'Don't hurt Annie.' Who is Annie?"

"I didn't say that. I said 'Patty.' I thought they were going to hurt Patty. So I started scratching them. I didn't know it was Jenny, I swear." My breath catches in my throat and I start breathing fast, quick, shallow breaths as I feel tears well up in my eyes. I sit back down and rub my eyes with my fists, pushing the tears back inside. *What is wrong with me?*

"Has that ever happened before?" Dr. Grenner asks.

"What?"

"A memory," she says, "while you were awake."

"I was just telling you about my dream," I argue.

"You left me for a moment there, you were in the memory. It must have felt so real," she soothes. "You looked like you were really scared. That must be an awful feeling."

"The monster was going to hurt her," I say.

"Annie?"

I nod. I can no longer hold back my tears; they escape and tickle my cheeks as they trickle down my face.

"Who is Annie?"

"I don't know. I don't know," I cry, slapping both hands against my thighs. "I don't know who Annie is!" I shout at her.

"What happened next?" she asks, calmly switching gears again. "At Jenny's house." She looks so calm and cool while I'm falling apart from the inside out.

"Jenny was fighting back and screaming, and a man came running into the room and grabbed me. He pulled me off Jenny."

"Who was it?"

"Jenny's dad," I answer.

"What did you do?"

"I bit his arm," I say, looking up into her face. "He was hurting me. He was going to hurt her. So I punched him. I swung both my fists against his chest and his face."

"You were screaming at him?"

"Yes, he was going to hurt her."

"Laney," Dr. Grenner says softly, "what were you screaming as you were punching Jenny's dad?"

"I—I—" I hesitate, afraid to say the words out loud. I remember that night so clearly; it was so awful. "I was yelling, 'Leave her alone! Take me instead!'"

CHAPTER 7

Danica

I t's starting to get dark, so I figure it's probably time to get home. "What time is it?" I ask, digging my feet into the sand and pushing my swing over toward Brent's. I reach him and grab on to the chain on his swing to pull myself closer. The chain is cold and feels good under my warm hands.

I take the beer from his hand and chug a couple of quick gulps. We are the only two people in the park and we have been sitting on the swings for hours, just talking. He takes another drink then tosses the empty through the air and it lands, clinking, on top of our other empties scattered at the base of a tree a few feet away. The tree is bare, aside from a few stubborn leaves that refuse to fall. The tree sways in the soft breeze, looking vulnerable and exposed, like a naked shadow of its former glory.

He holds out his wrist and I grab it to look at his watch. The light from the lamp post beside the swing set flicks on in response to the darkening skies and shines brightly from above, illuminating the face of his watch. "You like it?" he asks, smiling.

"Of course I like it," I say. "I'm the one who gave it to you." I smack him across the arm playfully. It was a gift for our six-month anniversary. It took me two months to save up for it with the money I stole from Benson's wallet.

"Oh yeah," he says, rubbing his chin and nodding like he's trying to draw a memory from the darkest corners of his mind. "It was you. That's why I haven't taken it off in a month, so that I'll always have a piece of you with me." He leans in and plants a gentle kiss on my cheek.

"Oh, such a sweet talker," I say, pulling away and pretending to be unmoved by his words, but my heart is dancing because I believe he means it.

"So, what time is it?" he asks.

"I didn't even notice." I laugh and pull his wrist back toward me. "Oh shoot," I say. "I have to go—I'm going to be late."

"I'll walk you," Brent says.

"No, you stay here, I'm good," I protest.

"I don't mind," he says.

"No, really, I'm good."

"This is weird, Danica," he argues. "We've been friends for years, dating for seven months and I have no idea where you even live. What's the big deal?"

"It's . . . it's complicated," I say. "It's just better this way. I have to go, though, seriously." I get up off my swing and notice that there is still one full beer left.

"Care if I drink this?" I ask, popping the top off and chugging before he answers.

"Why's your curfew so early anyway?" he asks. "You're almost seventeen and you have to be home by seven? That's messed up."

"Because Benson's a jerk," I say, wiping my mouth with the back of my hand. I raise the bottle to look at it: half left. I put it to my lips and gulp down the rest of it before Brent can ask for some.

"Well, can't you stay just a few more minutes?" he asks, smiling sneakily. "So I can at least say a proper goodnight?" He steps out of his swing and pulls me in toward him, gently knocking the bottle from my lips and licking a few drops of beer that are trickling down my chin.

I give him a quick kiss on the lips and pull away.

"Wait," he says, reaching for my shoulder. He misses, but his finger snags in the collar of my shirt, pulling it down a couple inches. I freeze and hope that it's too dark for him to have noticed, but when I see his eyes turn as big as saucers and a look of surprise erupts on his face I know he saw them.

"What the . . .?" he says, moving closer to me. "Why are you covered in bruises? Did someone hurt you?" He tries to pull at my shirt again, but I brush his hand away.

"It's nothing to worry about," I assure him. "I really have to go." I push away from him again and try to turn to leave. I feel tears spring up behind my eyes, threatening to erupt into a sea of sadness and despair. I need to get away from him. I break free from his grasp and start to run. I haven't cried in years and I'm afraid if I start, I'll probably never stop.

I hear his quick footsteps in the grass behind me. "Danica," he calls after only a few steps. I stop, because despite my protests to the name 'Danny' from the time I was a little girl, he is the only person in my life who actually calls me by my proper name. It's one of the many reasons why I love him. Another reason is that he has never tried to do anything more than hold my hand and kiss me. He talks to me and, as far as I can tell, really cares about me.

"Did someone hurt you?" he asks. His voice is quiet, barely above a whisper. He's standing in front of me now, a hand on each shoulder. I have to look up to meet his eyes as he's about half a foot taller than me. His eyes, a beautiful light hazel splattered with dark flecks, are fixed on mine with piercing intensity. He's squinting, just slightly, like he's concentrating and trying to read my thoughts. "Who hurt you?"

There are tears in his eyes now. Seeing him hurt for me breaks my heart and I can no longer hold the pain inside. I start to cry. Ball, actually. I cry so hard that within seconds I have snot dripping from my nose and I can't take a full breath, so I'm on the verge of hyperventilating.

Brent puts his arms around me and just holds me as my body jerks and heaves in his arms. I can feel his body shake slightly with his own tears, which makes me cry even harder.

Finally, after what feels like forever, I am out of tears. I stop crying and just stand there, wrapped in Brent's arms, wishing I could stay like this forever. I open my eyes and although they are blurry, I see that it is now pitch black, aside from the light from the lamps scattered throughout the park.

"I'm late," I say, trying to pull away. I wipe my nose with my sleeve and feel the snot go right through it.

"No," Brent says, "you can't leave like this. Please talk to me."

Because I feel so raw inside from the tears, I decide, for the first time in my life, to tell someone.

"It was Benson," I say and the tip of my secret explodes from my lips like a can of pop that has been shaken and popped open.

Brent pulls me into him and wraps his arms around me again. "Don't go home," he says.

"I have to."

"No, you don't. Come home with me. My parents can help you."

"I have to go home," I repeat.

"Why?"

"If I don't go home, he'll just go after my sister," I whisper.

"Your sister?" he asks. "You don't have a sister."

"I used to," I say. I picture Elly's face in my mind and I want to cry again, but I don't have any tears left.

"Where is she?" he asks.

"I don't know. But as long as I do what Benson says, then she's safe. If I don't do what he says, he will find her and hurt her, too. I can't let that happen."

"When was the last time you saw her?" he asks.

"A lifetime ago."

"How do you know she's okay?"

"I just know it. She has to be," I say. The one thing that keeps me going, keeps me from slitting my wrists to escape my own private hell, is the knowledge that I am keeping her safe. By going home every day, I am giving Elly the life she deserves, the life every little girl deserves. I am protecting her, like a good sister would.

"Have you ever tried to find her?" he asks.

I look up, startled. I have never even considered it. "No— no . . . I can't," I stammer. I can't let her see what has become of me.

"Don't you want to see for yourself that she's safe?"

"She's safe," I say forcefully. "I feel it in my heart." I look at him, anger building inside. She has to be safe, or my life is for nothing.

"Okay, okay," he says, wrapping his arms around me again, "I'm sorry. You're right. She's safe." He rubs my back and kisses the top of my head. "But you can't go home. We have to do something."

"No. There is nothing to do. He knows where she is and I don't. If I don't do what he says, he can find her. I wouldn't even be able to warn her." I feel my heart start to race again, fear building inside. "I'm going home." I turn and pull away from him. "I'll see you tomorrow," I say, and force a smile.

"Wait," he says. "I have something for you." He reaches into his pocket and pulls out a little box, which he holds atop his open palm as he pushes his hand toward me. "I was waiting for the perfect moment to give you this," he says. "I think the time is right now. You know I love you. I bought you this promise ring because I want you to know that I want to marry you one day. It's not much, but it's all I can afford right now. One day, I will buy you a real diamond ring."

I take the box and open it. Inside, nestled on a silver pillow, is a gold band with a small emerald centred between two tiny diamonds. It is the most beautiful ring I have ever seen. I take it from the box and with shaky hands, slip it onto my finger. It fits perfectly, like it was made just for me. The ring is warm; the heat extends over my fingers and up my arm, surrounding me with his love. In that moment, I know that for as long as I live, I will love no other.

I fall into his arms and kiss him. I feel his arms wrap around me, holding me tight against him.

"Don't go home," he pleads.

"I have to," I whisper.

He leans his forehead against mine and we stand in a trance-like state, lost together in a moment muddled somewhere between pure bliss and unspeakable fear.

"I'll see you tomorrow," I say and pull away from him, breaking our connection. He leaves his arms around me but loosens his grip to allow me to pull away from him. I take a few steps then turn to look back at him. Tears threaten again and my breath catches in my throat as I watch him standing there, looking sad and pathetic, like someone has just run over his favourite puppy.

I close my eyes to block him out, turn away, and start running. I almost laugh at the irony of my life as I run away from the only person who cares about me and I run toward my home, toward the beatings, the abuse and the hell that I know awaits me.

"You're late," Benson says when I open the front door slowly, trying to quietly sneak inside. He's sitting on a chair three feet from the door, facing it.

I let the screen door slam behind me.

"Um, yeah, sorry," I stammer. "I, uh, was at the library."

My head swings sideways as his palm connects with my cheek. I didn't even see it coming. I raise my own hand to my cheek to try to soothe the stinging and feel that my cheek is warm.

"You are lying, you little brat!" Benson yells. "You were out with your boyfriend, weren't you?" His eyes are wide, pupils dilated and he's jumpy. His right arm twitches as he yells.

"No," I protest, "I wasn't." I take small steps sideways, hoping to slip by him.

"You're lying, I can see it in your eyes," he yells in my face, squeezing my chin as he pulls my face close to his. His eyes are bloodshot, and he spits beer in my face as he speaks. "Did you let him touch you?" he snarls, pulling me in closer and sniffing around my face and neck.

He pushes me away from him, grunting in disgust. "Is this the kind of daughter you are raising, Crystal?" he shouts. "Is that the kind of mother you are, letting your kid run wild, doing whatever and whoever she wants?"

I look toward the living room, where Crystal is sitting, eyes barely open, with an almost empty bottle of vodka in her lap.

"Answer me!" he yells at her.

"No," she says quietly. "Listen to your father, Danny. Be a good girl and do what he says." She raises the bottle to her lips, and I see the vodka disappear, a big bubble flowing through the last of the alcohol before it quickly disappears down her throat. She puts the bottle down, and her eyes roll backwards before she closes them completely and topples over to the side, burying her face in a cushion.

"Yes, Danny, be a good girl and listen to your father," he repeats, sneering at me.

"You're not my father," I challenge. *I can't do this anymore. I want the life I could have with Brent.*

Whack. This time it's the back of his hand that connects with my face. "I'm tired of this bullshit, Danny. You're old news. Time for new blood." He looks at me, his eyes evil and dark. "Time for me to bring that sister of yours home and trade in your sorry ass."

"No!" I shriek. "No! I'm sorry. I'm sorry I was late—it'll never happen again. I'll do whatever you want. I'll be a good girl. I promise."

He's holding me by my collar, raising me up to him so that I'm standing on my tiptoes. "Last chance." He spits in my face. "Got it?"

"Let go of her!" I hear someone shout from outside. It's Brent. The door swings open and he's inside, tugging on my arm. "Let go of her!" he repeats.

Oh shit, he followed me home.

Benson lets go, pushing me toward Brent. Brent steps in front of me. I know he's trying to protect me, but he's a full foot shorter than Benson, and at least eighty pounds lighter. What can he do?

"At the library, were ya, Danny?" Benson laughs as he watches Brent raise his fists in a ready stance. We all know that Brent has zero chance of beating Benson in a fight, yet there he stands, willing to try. For me.

I watch Benson as he looks at Brent and I recognize the look that creeps up onto his face. He's staring at Brent like he has stared at a spider crawling across the living room floor, humouring it, letting it get to within inches of its destination before stomping, twisting and digging into it with his heel as he grinds the insect into the carpet.

There are now two people that I have to protect from Benson.

"It's up to you, Danny," Benson says. "Is it time for someone new?"

"No!" I shout, stepping out from behind Brent and placing myself between the two of them. "No!" I say again. "You have to leave, Brent," I say, turning to him. "I'm fine. Everything is good here, just a little misunderstanding. You have to leave and don't come back." I'm holding his hands in mine, squeezing them as I force the words out.

"Danica," Brent pleads, "don't do this."

I can't bring myself to look into his eyes, so I keep my head down as I twist his ring off my finger and force back the tears that are threatening to come.

I feel Benson's smirk from behind my back and it makes me hate him even more. I feel his evilness engulf me, choke the life out of me and turn my heart black.

This is the only way I can think of to keep Brent from becoming a spider beneath Benson's heel. The only way I can think of to protect Brent is to send him away, too.

"Go," I say, holding the ring out to him, forcing it into his hand when he refuses to take it, "and don't ever talk to me again."

CHAPTER 8

Elaina

"Hi, Mom," I shout, walking into our living room. Dad's car isn't in the driveway like it usually is when I get home from soccer practice. "Mom?" I shout upstairs. I listen for her usual response, but there is none. Instead I hear Max's footsteps before I see him round the corner. "Come on, boy," I say and pat my shins to call him over. When he sees me, he starts sprinting toward me and then chases me as I take the stairs two at a time to my parents' bedroom and find it empty. "Mom? Dad? Anybody home?" I shout as I go back downstairs carrying Max. I pet his head while he licks my face as I walk through the house looking for a note to tell me where they are.

I worry for a moment that something is wrong because I've never come home to an empty house with no explanation. But then I decide that if something were wrong, Dad would have phoned me.

I realize that this is the opportunity I've been waiting for for months, to have both Mom and Dad out of the house so I can check through their room. I have to move quickly because they could walk through the door at any second, so I dig through all the drawers and the closet as fast as I can. Even Mom's bedside table doesn't give up any secrets. Disappointed, I decide it's time to search the last room in the house that I haven't looked through yet.

I tiptoe down to the basement. It's ridiculous, but I'm always a little bit afraid to go into the basement by myself. *Another repressed childhood memory?* I wonder and laugh at myself. Our basement is just a big room with a couch and television, some workout equipment in one corner, including a treadmill that is always covered in drying laundry. It's all open and bright because of the big windows that Dad had put in a few years ago after a family in our neighbourhood died in a fire because their basement windows were too small for them to climb through, so I'm not quite sure why I'm such a chicken.

There's a furnace room and bathroom off to the side and behind the furnace is a dark, spooky storage room. It was supposed to be a cold storage for food, but we never used it, so it became the place where things went when they were no longer needed or wanted and there was nowhere else to put them.

I shiver as I twist the doorknob. I can feel the cold from the room coming out from under the door. I quickly pull the string to turn on the light once I'm inside and I leave the door open, both so that I can hear if Mom and Dad come home and because I'm afraid I'll get claustrophobic if I close myself in here. Even with Max here with me, I don't like this room.

I wave my hands in front of my face and over my head to knock away the cobwebs. There's an old bike, scooter and helmet in one corner, remnants from my childhood I assume, although I don't know why they would keep those particular items when I've had at least five bikes and scooters throughout my life. *Maybe they were my first ones? Could be—they're small enough for me to have used them when I was only two or three.*

There's a pantry-style closet and when I open it, I see it's filled with little girl clothes and toys. I dig through the shelves but don't find anything of interest. There's a pile of boxes against the wall, half of them labelled "Nancy – Skinny Clothes" the other half labelled "Nancy – Fat Clothes." I pull them down and quickly dig through them just to make sure the labels aren't meant to deter anyone digging for secrets. They're not; all that's in them are old, ugly clothes.

Thank God Mom never gave me any of her hand-me-downs like Patty's mom gave to her. I laugh, remembering all the times Jenny and I laughed at Patty when she showed up at school wearing old lady clothes. She finally begged her mother to stop making her wear her old clothes and after threatening to go to school naked rather than wear another hand-me-down, Patty's mother finally relented.

There's another pile of boxes, these ones unlabelled. I pull down the first one and look through old dishes and frying pans. The next one has an old coffee maker, in pieces, obviously broken. *Why are they keeping all this crap?* I wonder. After digging through three more boxes of broken or old appliances I'm ready to give up.

There's only one box left, and I pull it out expecting more crap, but my heart starts racing when I see it's a box full of files. I flip through the files; they're labelled "Taxes 2005," "House," and "Insurance." I quickly dig through each file and toss them aside. I pull out the next one, labelled "Rebecca." My heart jumps, skipping a beat and I start shaking as I reach out my hand to open the file. Just then my phone rings in my pocket, scaring the crap out of me. "Ahh!" I scream and jump. I ignore it, deciding that this file is more important. But it doesn't stop ringing, so I sit and wait for it to stop. Finally, after about the twentieth ring, I figure it must be important. *Probably Jenny with another fashion crisis or Patty with boyfriend troubles,* I decide.

I pull the phone from my pocket and answer it quickly when I see "Dad" on the screen.

"Hello."

"Laney, it's Dad. Mom's been admitted to the hospital. You have to come right away. Fourth floor. I've sent a cab for you; it'll be there in two minutes. I have to go." *Click.*

Mom!

I keep the file out and throw everything back into the box. Then I pile the boxes back up. They're crooked, but I don't care. I take the file, pull the light string and close the door behind me. I race up the stairs and see the cab pulling into the driveway. I grab my soccer bag and pull out my cleats, tossing them on the floor in the hallway. I stuff the file inside, throw the strap over my shoulder and race out to the cab.

"Where is she?" I ask, running up to the desk on the fourth floor of the hospital. "My mother, where is she?"

"What's her name?" the woman sitting at the desk asks. She looks up at me from her computer screen and looks genuinely concerned.

"Nancy, Nancy Samson," I say, out of breath.

"Laney," I hear. I look up and see Dad coming out of a room down the hall. He reaches me within a few seconds and hugs me. "She's in here," he says. "She's asking for you."

"What's wrong?" I ask. "Is she going to be okay?" He keeps his arm around me as we walk down the hall, toward the room he just came from.

Two people in scrubs run past us and almost bump into me. A woman walks by, pushing an older man in a wheelchair. He's slumped over, leaning to one side. I shiver as I look at him and wonder if that's what you look like just before you die.

"She's sick," Dad says. "I don't know, it doesn't look good. She wants to see you."

We stop in the doorway and look inside. Mom is hooked up to a bunch of wires and an IV is dripping liquid into her through a tube. Her brown hair, normally shiny and smooth, is dull and straw-like. The bleached white of the hospital gown makes her face look pale and ghostly. Her arms look thin, just skin-covered bone. *Was she always this thin?* I wonder, realizing that I hadn't been paying much attention to her lately. She was always lying in bed and I was busy with school and soccer, friends and Norman, my new boyfriend. A wave of guilt washes over me as I realize I've been a horrible daughter, and judging by the way she looks, it might be too late for me to ever make it up to her.

"I—I can't go in there," I say, trying to turn and back away.

"You have to, sweetie," Dad says. "She's asking for you. I have to go talk to the nurse—I have to find out what they know. I'll be right back. She shouldn't be alone. It's okay, you go inside," he says, gently shoving me inside the room and whispering, "Honey, Laney's here to see you," before he turns to leave.

"Mom," I say quietly, moving slowly toward her bed. Her breathing is heavy and raspy. There's an empty bed beside her, a curtain pulled open beside it. I can see the lake from the window and a few seagulls soaring over the water. "Mom," I repeat.

"Sweetie," she says, opening her eyes a crack. She raises her hand up toward me.

I move forward quickly and take her hand. "Mom," I say meekly.

"I'm so happy to see you, Rebecca," she says. "I was so scared I'd never see you again."

"I'm here, Mom. It's me, Laney," I say.

She looks confused. "Laney?"

"Yes, Mom, it's me, Laney." I squeeze her hand.

"No," she says. She looks confused and her eyes start shifting, looking back and forth across the room. The beeps on the monitor quicken. "No," she says again. The beeps quicken even more. I look up toward the door, hoping my dad will walk back through it, or a nurse, anyone.

I'm starting to freak out. "Hello!" I shout toward the door. No one answers. I feel Mom start to shake, her hand trying to pull away from me.

"No, no," she's repeating. She looks scared and is trying to pull away from me. I'm afraid she's going to fall out of her bed.

"Sorry," I say. "Mom, it's me—it's Rebecca," I lie. Unsure what to do, I place both my hands on her face and turn her toward me, so I can look into her eyes. "It's okay, I'm here, Mom. I'm Rebecca. I'm here with you." I rub her shoulders as I keep my eyes locked on hers, trying to calm her. Meanwhile my mind is racing.

The beeps slow down and she looks at me. "Rebecca?" she asks. "Is that really you, Rebecca?"

"Yes, Mom, it's Rebecca. I came here to see you," I say. *Who the heck is Rebecca?*

"Oh, baby," Mom says, raising her hand to my face, then starts petting my head like I'm a puppy. "Oh, baby," she repeats, "I didn't think I was ever going to see you again."

"I didn't mean to scare you, Mom. I'm right here, right by your side. It's okay, everything is okay." I force my voice to sound smooth and comforting even though a lump of panic is rising in my throat. I grab her hand and hold it in mine.

"Oh, baby, I'm sorry," she says. "I'm so sorry." She starts crying, her body jiggling, slowly at first, then her whole body starts to shake, and tears trickle down her cheeks. "Is it really you?" she asks.

"Yes, Mom, it's really me," I say. "I'm right here." I lean into her again so she can focus on my face.

"Oh," Mom says. She looks confused. "I thought I'd lost you. I didn't think I'd ever see you again. I'm sorry, Rebecca," she cries. She pulls me in even closer, her eyes locked on mine. As she stares at me, I see her expression change and her eyes widen. "I couldn't save you!" she shouts, sitting up suddenly. A wire pulls loose, the monitors start beeping like crazy. "I couldn't save you!" she shouts again and sits up as she pushes me away.

"Dad!" I yell toward the doorway. "Dad!"

"Nooo! Nooo!" Mom is screaming. "I'm so sorry, Rebecca!"

"Nancy!" Dad shouts, running into the room behind a nurse. The nurse puts her hand on Mom's shoulder, "It's okay, Mrs.

Samson," the nurse comforts. "Just lie back, it's okay." Mom continues to struggle, fighting to stay sitting up.

I jump up toward Dad and he wraps his arms around me.

"No!" Mom screams again, her arms outstretched toward me. "I couldn't save you! I couldn't save you!"

The beeps stop suddenly and turn into one constant stream of noise as Mom falls backwards limply onto her bed.

"Take her outside," the nurse shouts at Dad, pressing a button on Mom's bed.

As Dad pulls me out of the room two nurses run in, pushing past us. Before he drags me around the corner, I see one nurse climb up onto Mom's bed and start pressing down repeatedly on her chest, just like I had practiced in gym class, when we had to learn how to do CPR.

"Is she going to die?" I cry.

"I hope not," Dad says. He puts his arm around my shoulder and pulls me into him. I rest my head against his shoulder and let my tears fall.

We sit there in silence for what feels like forever. Finally, when I don't have any tears left, I ask, "Who's Rebecca?"

"I don't know, honey."

Doctors and nurses rush in and out of Mom's room.

"She called me Rebecca and said she buried me," I sniff and wipe the back of my wrist across my nose. "I don't know what she means."

"I told you," Dad says, "she's sick, honey. She doesn't know what she says."

We stand there, watching doctors and nurses running in and out of Mom's room. Machines are beeping. The intercom is paging doctors. Everyone who runs toward her room looks panicked and everyone who comes out of it looks defeated. Eventually, people stop running toward her room and the only trickle of people are the doctors and nurses who walk out of her room, look up toward us but don't meet our eyes as they walk quickly past us.

"I'm sorry, Mr. Samson," a doctor says, coming out of Mom's room. His head is lowered and he's shaking it slightly side to side. "Your wife is gone. We need you to come with us."

"No!" I yell, feeling my body go limp. I lean into Dad for support and he keeps me from crumpling to the ground.

"It's okay," Dad says, holding me up. "Go sit down there." He points to the waiting area. "I'll be right back." He kisses the top of my head and pushes me gently toward the waiting area then he follows the doctor. "I'll be right back," he says again.

I stand there for a moment, frozen. Mom's been so sick for so long that she hasn't really been a part of our lives for years. But just knowing she was up in her room if I wanted to see her was a comfort. A pang of guilt washes over me again as I realize how little I went up to spend time with her. Now she was gone; I'd never be able to climb into bed beside her, put my arms around her and just hold her as she cried. I never understood why she was always so sad. I never understood why she was so sick. Now I never will.

I turn and go to the waiting area as directed. I sit, bury my face in my hands and let a fresh wave of tears pour out.

I feel something touch my foot and look up.

"I'm sorry," a nurse says, "you left this in your mother's room. I brought it out for you in case you needed it." She looks down at my soccer bag that she's placed by my feet. She smiles at me—a soft, sad smile—and turns away.

The file.

I open my bag and pull out the file. There are pictures of a little girl. Pictures of her as a newborn with Mom and Dad smiling happily into the camera as they hold her close to them. Pictures of her as a baby, sitting up with a big, gummy grin and a stuffed bear beside her. Pictures of her as a little girl, maybe two or three years old.

There's artwork—scribbles, really—crayon scrolled across pieces of paper in random colours and movements. Put away safely forever in this file like they're lost treasures. Behind the pictures, behind the artwork, behind the little crafts that had been saved, there's a piece of paper, an official certificate. I read it, but don't understand its meaning. My brain can't make sense of what's on the certificate.

I see Dad come out of the room and walk toward me, so I fold up the paper and tuck it into my back pocket.

Who is she? I wonder, seeing the little girl's face in my mind.

More importantly, where is she?

CHAPTER 9

Danica

The relief of finishing my last day of high school vanishes the moment my hand grasps the doorknob. My stomach turns and I'm hit with a wave of nausea. *Something feels different,* I think as I turn the knob and push through the door.

"Congratulations, Danny," Benson slurs, when I walk through the door. "You graduated. It's about time." He laughs, a drunken, sloppy laugh, and raises a beer bottle toward me. He's sitting on a recliner chair, feet up, in front of the television. There are empty bottles in a pile on the floor, an empty chip bag on his lap, and chip crumbs across his bare chest.

"Where's Crystal?" I ask, looking around.

"Time to start earning your keep," he says.

"Where's Crystal?" I repeat. Her usual spot on the couch is empty. As much as I've always hated seeing her sitting on the couch, in various stages of inebriation, not seeing her there is worse. "Is she okay?" I ask, forcing myself not to panic. She's never been much of a mother, but she's all I have. If she's not here, Benson won't have to wait until she passes out, won't have to hide what he does to me.

I've never really been sure if he's so good at hiding it that Crystal doesn't actually know or whether she just pretends not to know. Either way, it's meant that I at least get a few hours after school, before Crystal passes out drunk on the couch religiously around ten o'clock each night, before I have to worry about the dreaded footsteps coming toward my room. "Where is she?" I ask sharply.

"Relax," he says, "she's in bed."

Relief washes over me as I look upstairs toward her bedroom.

"Why?" A fresh wave of panic rushes over me. She has not slept in her room for over a decade. I haven't even seen her bedroom in all that time as the door was always kept shut and Benson warned me that I'd be sorry if I ever went snooping around in there. I was already sorry for enough, I didn't need to add that to the list, so I stayed out.

"I told you," he sneers, "it's time for you to earn your keep. I can't have her in the way. I gave her some medicine and sent her to bed," he says. "Now go up to your room."

He's looking at me strangely, pure evil in his eyes. The hairs on the back of my neck stand up and my pulse quickens. *Something is not right.* I walk quickly through the living room, heart pounding in my chest. There is a pill bottle, spilled over with a few pills spread out around it on the coffee table and at least half a dozen empty beer bottles.

I creep up the stairs to Crystal's bedroom door, which is open just a crack. I peer inside and see her passed out, face down on the bed. There's another empty beer bottle on the floor beside where her fingers hang lifelessly, and a man passed out on the bed beside her. I'm momentarily shocked by how dirty the room is; clothes and garbage literally cover every inch of the floor and there's a spot of mold growing in the far corner and under the windowsill.

"Crystal," I say, pushing through the door. She doesn't move so I walk up and shake her. "Crystal!" I shout.

"Huh, wha—?" She raises her head just slightly off the bed and looks at me. Her eyes are bloodshot, her hair is ratty and knotted and her bangs are hanging down in her face. Her makeup is smudged into dark circles around her eyes.

"I need your help," I say. She stares at me blankly. "Please, Mom," I add, hoping to appeal to her non-existent maternal instincts.

She responds, but not in the way I was hoping.

"My baby girl," she says. "Is that you, my baby girl?" She lifts her arm and reaches out toward me as her face contorts into a scrunched-up pout. A tear squeezes out from the corner of her eye and trickles down her cheek. "I missed you so much," she says.

"It's me, Danica. I need your help," I plead. I'm so creeped out my stomach is twisting into knots and I've started to sweat. Benson is up to something worse than usual; I can feel it.

"Where's my baby girl?" she asks. She's sitting up now, her body trembling. She's looking all around the room, at me, around me, behind her. She looks panicked, like a wild animal that's been cornered. "Where's my baby girl?" she shrieks as she stands up and comes toward me with both arms outstretched.

The sudden movement and her weird rambling startle me and I step away from her. "Mom, it's me, Danica," I say firmly. "I need you to focus."

Benson pushes me aside, knocking me into the dresser. He wraps his arms around her like he's a straitjacket. He's holding her arms down by her side as she struggles to get away. "You're sick," he says. "You need more medicine." He keeps his arms wrapped around her as he takes a couple steps with her, leading her back to the bed. He sits her down and opens his palm, holding out two little white pills for her.

"Don't take them, Mom," I plead. "I need you!" I shriek, watching in desperation as I know my only hope is really no hope at all.

I lunge toward her, but Benson shoves me aside with an easy swipe of his arm and I fall to the floor.

"Please don't take those, Mom," I whisper from the floor, the words barely escaping my lips. I know with total certainty that she is going to take them and nothing I say will convince her to help me. *What help could she be anyway?* I laugh at the irony. I've been more of a mother to her the last ten years than she's ever been to me.

She looks at me and keeps watching me as she takes the pills from his hand and swallows them, downing them with the beer that Benson hands her. After she tilts her head back and swallows, she looks at me again. Her eyes are red, like she's been crying, but there are no tears. She's pale and gaunt. She looks like a zombie, sitting there staring at me like she's thinking, or trying to remember something.

"I'm so sorry, Danny," she whispers. "Take care of my baby girl for me." Then she closes her eyes and lets herself fall backwards onto the bed beside the lifeless body of the random man who has not moved an inch this whole time, despite all the movement and shouting.

Benson turns and stares at me. If looks could kill, I would be lying on the floor drowning in a pool of my own blood. I've never seen so much hatred in one look before.

I turn and run straight into my bedroom, closing the door quickly behind me. I keep my hand on the doorknob and lean my head toward my door, trying to keep the room from spinning. *I've got to get out of here.*

"It's about time," I hear a gruff voice say behind me. I turn and look to see a naked, hairy man sitting on my bed. He's probably about fifty years old and has a beer belly. The top of his head is bald, and he's got a really bad comb-over. His gaze is transfixed on a pair of handcuffs that are dangling from his hand.

I open my door and go to step out. Benson is standing in my doorway, arms folded across his chest. "Where do you think you're going?" he asks.

"Mom!" I shout. The room is spinning. There's nowhere to go. I consider jumping out my window, even willing to risk a broken leg, but it's closed and locked and there's no way I could get it open and push through the screen before Benson could stop me. And then he'd be pissed. *Maybe I could just jump through the glass.* "I need to talk to Mom," I say, forcing a steady voice to try to exude a non-existent confidence. *Maybe I can reason with him if I just stay calm.*

"It's okay, sweetie," Benson says in his creepy sing-song voice. "You don't need Mommy, I'm here." He unfolds his arms and I see that he's holding his phone, set to video recording.

"Mom!" I shout again.

"Shhh!" he sputters, spitting beer into my face. "I told you she's sick. I'm all that you need." He's still singing the words, like he's trying to comfort a scared child. He steps forward, toward me. When I don't move, he bumps me, pushing me back into my room, and closes the door behind him. He takes a drink from a bottle of vodka and puts it down at his feet.

"I told you, sweetie, it's time to start earning your keep now that you're done school. I don't want no freeloader living in my house. I've taken care of you all these years, now it's time for you to start taking care of me. You hear me? Things cost money, you know. You think this house is free, you think the food I give you is cheap? No sireee, it's time you started contributing around here."

"No," I say, "please no."

"Okay," he says, "backing away from me. Whatever you say, sweetheart."

For a moment I can breathe again. I take a step toward the window. *How hard would I have to hit the window in order to break through the glass?* I wonder. I look over at the man on my bed. He's staring at me like I'm a wounded deer and he's a hungry wolf, like he knows I won't put up much of a fight. I take another, faster step toward the window.

"You wait here while I go get Elly," Benson says. I stop my step in mid-air and stumble, bumping into my dresser. When I regain my balance and look back at him he's got his hand on the doorknob, turning it. "She won't give me any backtalk," he says. "Elly's a good girl. I saw her today, you're sister. She's cute. I sat in front of her house and watched her as she walked to school. I can pick her up any time I want and bring her back here to replace you." He's looking at me now, eyes fixed on mine. He doesn't blink, but his eyes are squinted, barely open. I can still feel the daggers he's shooting out of them pierce my skin and spread poison throughout my body. Just feeling his eyes on me makes my skin crawl like there are a thousand centipedes fighting just beneath the surface.

"No, you didn't," I argue. I'm trying to sound brave, like I'm not afraid of him, but I curse myself when my voice cracks. I look down at his vodka and wish I could grab the bottle and take a sip, just enough to give me some courage.

"Oh yes, I did. I followed her in my car the whole way. She was walking with a friend—she didn't even notice me." When he smiles and licks his lips my stomach wrenches and I feel bile rise into my mouth. I gag as I swallow it back down. I can't tell if he's telling the truth or full of shit. *Can I call his bluff?*

"No!" I shout.

"What's that?" he asks, a wicked smile creeping across his ugly face.

"I'll do it," I say.

"You'll do what?" he asks, pushing the screen on his phone and raising it to my face.

"I'll do whatever you want," I say into the camera.

"Beg for it," he says.

"What?"

"Look into the camera and beg for it. Make me believe you want it," he says. He covers his hand over his phone and whispers,

"If I don't believe you, I'm going to go get that cute sister of yours to replace you."

He raises the camera back up to my face.

"Please," I say.

He raises his face from behind the camera and looks at me, raising one eyebrow. He has dirty sweat dripping from his hairline and pooling above his eyebrows. He smiles slightly and his face disappears behind his camera phone again.

"I'll do whatever you want."

I have to keep her safe. Nothing else matters.

Then he raises a hand to me and opens up his palm. There is a single pill in his hand. I don't know what it is, and I don't care. I grab the pill and reach down for the bottle of vodka. I close my eyes as I wash the pill down, chugging down as much of the burning liquid as I can. I wait for my throat to stop burning then I raise the bottle and take another big gulp as I step toward my bed.

The man is smiling nervously, eyes shifting back and forth between me and Benson. He's playing with the handcuffs, flipping one of the locking arms around and around. I hold out my right hand to him. He snaps the cuff on and squeezes it tight. I can see it digging into my skin. He lifts my arm to the frame of the top bunk and slips the empty cuff over the rail.

Benson's smiling now; he looks alive and excited, or high and drunk. Maybe both. He holds the camera up, looks through the screen then moves his face to the side, then back behind his camera again. He takes two steps to the side and does the same thing. Apparently satisfied with the view he now has on his camera screen, he whistles and says, "It's showtime, baby."

CHAPTER 10

Elaina

"Skipping soccer again?" Norman asks, running up behind me.

"Yeah," I say.

"How come?" he asks, falling into step beside me.

"Don't feel like it," I say, and continue looking straight ahead.

"Where you headed?" he asks.

"Just going to wander for a bit," I say.

"Can I wander with you?"

"Whatever."

"You okay?" he asks. He reaches up and touches my arm.

Startled, I shake him off at first. "Sorry," I say, finally looking at him. "You got your hair cut," I blurt, when I finally look at him. He wore his dark hair short and got it cut all the time. He's wearing a navy blue sweatshirt and jeans.

"You like?" he asks, red colouring rising into his cheeks.

I laugh. "Of course," I say, "it looks the same as it always does." I laugh again. He is goofy and sweet and very handsome. And for some reason he has willingly dated me for over a year, despite my moods and apparent craziness.

"There's the smile I love so much," he says and leans in to give me a quick kiss on the cheek.

He pulls out a bouquet of flowers from behind his back and holds them out to me.

"Not for you," he says when I smile and reach for them. "I thought we could walk over to the cemetery and put them at your mom's grave."

My smile disappears. "I'm not going to the cemetery."

"It's a year today, right?" he asks. "That's the real reason you're skipping soccer?"

Damn.

I nod, turning away from him again and continue walking. We walk in silence, each footstep hitting the ground in sync and by the time we reach the cemetery I'm not sure whether I've led him there or he has led me there, but I am overwhelmed with a feeling of comfort and calm knowing he is beside me. Aside from the day of her funeral, I have never visited my mom's grave.

It is foggy and cool. The clouds are dark, like they could sprout rain at any moment. The fog makes the cemetery seem spooky and ominous as we weave our way through headstone-laden gravesites. It's the perfect weather for a cemetery visit.

Was it my fault she was sick? Was it my fault she died?

My breath catches as we reach her headstone. Norman hands the bouquet of flowers to me. I take them and quickly bend, placing them at the base of her headstone, then take my place beside him again. There is another bouquet beside the one I placed there, a collection of large lilies and daisies, tied together with a bright yellow ribbon. We stand in silence, staring at her grave.

I picture her screaming at me, "I couldn't save you!" right before her heart stopped. I shake my head; my last memory of her is too painful to think about. I had ignored it for the last year. But standing here, staring at her final resting place, it all comes rushing back.

"Who's Rebecca?" I had asked my dad, tears streaming down my face.

"I don't know, honey," Dad had said, keeping his arms wrapped around me.

Doctors and nurses rushed in and out of Mom's room.

"She said she buried me. I don't know what she meant."

"I told you," Dad said. "She's sick, honey. She doesn't know what she's saying."

Eventually the doctors and nurses who left her room didn't come rushing back. Finally, there was only one doctor left; he stepped out of her room and stopped in front of us. "I'm sorry, Mr. Samson," he said. "Your wife is gone. We need you to come with us."

A single tear escapes and trickles down my cheek now, falling into the grass at my feet, as I recall the doctor's words. Norman puts his hand on my back, bringing my thoughts back to the present.

"You ready?" he asks.

I nod.

He takes my hand and starts leading me away. I turn for a final look at my mom's grave and notice a bright yellow ribbon dancing gently in the soft breeze a few hundred feet away, peeking out from behind a full leafy bush.

"Wait," I say, pulling away from him and walking quickly over to the ribbon. It is a replica of the bouquet at my mom's grave. It's away from the other headstones, inside the forest that borders the cemetery and hidden behind a wall of brush. If it hadn't been breezy I wouldn't have noticed it. I wonder if the wind had blown it into the forest, but it is propped perfectly up against the tree and behind the bushes, so I realize it had to have been placed there. I look around but don't see any other headstones. I kneel and look inside at the words scribbled on the card inside the bouquet:

Beloved Angel Rebecca Dawn

I've seen that name before. It was on the document in the file, the one I found when I was waiting for Dad in the hospital.

Behind the pictures of a little girl, behind the scribble drawings and collection of crafts obviously made by a little kid, there was one official document, a Change of Name Certificate confirming a successful application for change of name of the individual from "Rebecca Dawn Samson" to "Elaina Dawn Samson." I hadn't known what it meant, couldn't comprehend it, so I had tucked it away in my pocket. Back home, I had hidden it away in my bottom drawer, in the back behind my too-small jeans that never left the drawer. I had put it there and forgotten about it. Like the last memory of my mother, it was too hard to think about. It was too much for my brain to try to understand.

"Who's that?" Norman asks, stepping beside me and reading the card.

"I have no idea," my mind is racing. *Rebecca? I'm Rebecca? No. I was Rebecca? No. I have a sister Rebecca? Yes, that feels right for some reason, I have a sister. No, had a sister,* I correct remembering the card, *but that doesn't feel right anymore. I am going crazy.*

Suddenly, another name pops into my head: *Annie.*

I pull out my phone and snap a picture of the card and the bouquet, then tuck my phone back into my pocket.

"I have to go," I say, turning suddenly and running. I run all the way out of the cemetery, down the road, and around the block. Norman stays beside me, matching my pace step for step.

"I'm going crazy," I say when I finally stop. I'm crying. *For my mother? For the sister I didn't know? For Annie?*

"Who is Annie?" I hear Dr. Grenner's voice in my head ask me.

"Hey," Norman says, "this is a tough day, it's okay to cry, it doesn't mean you're going crazy." He leans in and hugs me, squeezing me close to him and I feel myself start to calm down.

"Look," he says, pointing. "This'll make you feel better. Come with me," he says, taking my hand and leading me toward a playground.

The playground is empty, aside from a man walking a large white dog along the perimeter of the park.

"Here," Norman says, taking my hand and leading me to the swing set. There are two regular swings and a baby swing.

"Sit," he says, "I'll push you."

"This is ridiculous," I say, protesting. "I'm too old for this." I can't help but laugh, though, when I look at Norman. He looks so excited and childlike with his huge grin and green eyes sparkling.

At first, I force a laugh, not wanting to disappoint him. But soon I'm laughing for real, enjoying the feel of the wind blowing through my hair as he pushes me higher and higher. I'm squeezing the chains tightly and leaning way back, pumping my legs to force myself so high I feel like I'm flying. My eyes are shut and I'm soaring through the air.

"Higher, Annie!" I shout and as soon as the words are out, my legs stop pumping and dangle lifelessly below me. I feel like I'm spinning, like I'm going to throw up, as a feeling of déjà vu overtakes me. I open one hand and lose the grip on the chain, half-falling and twisting as the swing still flies through the air, twisting close to the bar.

"Whoa!" Norman shouts. "Hey, I gotcha." He grabs me, slowing the swing down. "Too much for you?" He laughs. "Maybe I should have put you in the baby swing," he teases.

I force another laugh, but my head's still spinning, I'm still trying to figure out what is wrong with me. *I'm headed to a mental institution for sure,* I think, and I have a sudden urge to be back in Dr. Grenner's office, lying down on her couch this time.

"Let's try the slide," he says, happily tugging me along. I climb the ladder behind him and follow him to the slide like I'm in a trance. "Let's make a train," he says, patting the spot behind where he's sitting, calling me to join him. "My brother and I used to do this when we were little. Come on, it'll be fun," he urges.

I close my eyes and sit behind him, my stomach still reeling. I put one leg on either side of him and he grabs my feet, pulling them up onto his thighs. "Hold on," he says so I wrap my arms around his neck, squeezing and digging my face into his back.

"Too tight," he complains, peeling my arms away and placing them around his belly. "Like this," he says.

Everything starts spinning again, wildly this time. I pull my arms away from him. I lean over the slide and throw up as we whip down the slide.

Elly Belly, I hear a voice whisper.

"What'd you call me?" I ask, stepping out from behind him at the bottom, wiping my mouth with my sleeve.

"What?" he says. "I didn't call you anything. I just moved your arms because you were strangling me." He laughs, standing up and coming over to me. "Are you okay?"

I'm twirling around, looking for someone. *Who called me that?* I hear a girl's voice; she's laughing. *Come on, Elly Belly! Come down the slide with me.*

It's Annie.

"Annie!" I scream. "Where are you, Annie?"

"Hey," Norman says, grabbing my arm.

I look straight at him, but I don't see him. Instead I see myself as a little girl, tucked behind another girl almost identical to me, at the top of the slide. "Ready! One, two, three. Let's go!" she shouts and we're off, giggling as we zip to the bottom.

She stops laughing at the bottom and I'm not sure why, until I notice her looking up, talking to a man. I hide behind her back, afraid, but when I hear him ask how old we are I'm excited because I just had a birthday. "I'm three," I say, popping out from behind her to show the man my hand with three fingers outstretched.

She talks to him a little more and I stay behind her back. Then I feel Annie tugging on me; she pulls me out from behind her and shoves me toward the man. "Take her," she says to him. "Her name is Elaina."

I look back at Annie, my eyes wide with fear. "You'll be okay," she whispers. "He'll keep you safe. I love you, Elly Belly," she says. "Always remember that."

I take the man's hand and walk with him, away from Annie. When we reach the edge of the park, I look up at him.

Smiling down at me, I see Daddy's loving face.

CHAPTER 11

Danica

"There you are," a male voice says.

I know who it is before I even turn around. "Brent," I whisper. His name on my lips instantly lifts my mood. "What are you doing here?" I force myself to remain calm even though I want to jump up, throw my arms around him and tell him how much I love him and miss him. I want to tell him I was stupid for giving his ring back and ignoring him every time we met in the hallway at school. I want to tell him I've gone crazy every single day that he's been away at college and beg him to give me the ring back so we can have the future he promised me.

Instead, I keep my eyes focused on the grass and continue swaying slowly on the swing. The only one holding me back from living the life of my dreams is me, and Benson's threat of finding Elly and hurting her the way he's hurt me. Sometimes I wish I could hate her, to put my safety before hers. *Maybe it was her turn to protect me, to give me a chance at happiness.*

No, I snap to myself, *it's my job, my only job, to protect her and to love her. It's a promise I made and will keep until the day I die.*

"Looking for you," he says. He comes around from behind me, takes my hand and pulls me up off the swing and into a hug. "I thought I'd find you here."

I could stay wrapped up in his arms forever.

"It's my favourite place," I say remembering all the hours we spent together in the park, holding hands, talking, planning a future that could never be. I wrap my arms tight around his neck and feel his arms squeeze me to him. It feels so good to be near him again, to feel his warm breath on my neck as he hugs me.

The sun comes out from behind a cloud and makes the entire park shine. A little girl chases a puppy and squeals with delight when she catches it, rolling in the grass with it as both parents watch over her, smiling. I smile, too, imagining Elly as that little girl. I know she's almost a grown woman now, but in my mind, she will always be a little girl. I want to cry for everything in her life that I've missed. But my heart is happy for every pain that I've saved her from, and I know that if I had to do it all again, I would do the same thing. I feel good knowing that I've protected her, I've been a good big sister, just like I promised our dad I would be before he left.

Then I remember my own life, what Benson has turned me into and I'm ashamed. I pull away, embarrassed, afraid Brent will find out the truth about me.

The sun disappears behind another cloud, casting a shadow over the park, over my secrets.

"Wait," he says, catching my hand and holding me in place. "I just got back. I really missed you. I just want to see you." His voice rises, like he's still a nervous teenager. But he doesn't look like the boy I knew, the boy who turned and walked away with tears in his eyes when I stood between him and Benson and told him to go away and never talk to me again. He's a man now, taller, stronger, his face more mature. And so handsome. *How could I have let him walk out of my life?*

"Oh yeah," I say, pretending I'd forgotten he's been away at school, like imagining him every single night living the life of a single, carefree college student didn't rip my heart to shreds over and over again. "How was your first year of college?"

"A big party," he says, laughing.

I sit back down on the swing and he sits on the one beside me. We sway slowly beside each other, hand in hand, like we had done so many times when we were dating. There's awkwardness to our touch now; our hands fumble against the other's, trying to find the fit that came so naturally before.

I picture him living on his own, away from the watchful eyes of his parents, partying every night with the pretty college girls. I want to curl up into a ball and die.

"How have you been?" he asks. He looks straight into my eyes, like he's trying to read my mind, like he's trying to get me to answer the real question, the one he's too afraid to ask.

"Okay," I say, looking away. *He can't know the truth.* "How long are you back for?" I ask, hoping to change the subject.

"Just the summer," he says. "I got a job at the hardware store. They're looking for more help—maybe you can get a job there, too," he says excitedly. "You know, so we can see each other there."

I smile; I can't help it. Brent is the only person who is genuinely happy at the thought of seeing me. I feel a pain in my heart. I know Benson will never let me work at the hardware store.

"Yeah, maybe," I say and shrug. "I've never had a job, though." *Not one I can put on a resumé at least.* "I doubt they'd hire me."

"Well, it's worth a shot," he says. "I mean, if you want to," he adds. The space between us has turned awkward. We turn away from each other, but keep our hands locked.

Birds chirp and flutter from tree to tree. A squirrel scurries past us and climbs the tree closest to us, causing a robin to squawk and dive-bomb it to chase it away from its nest. Buds are erupting on the branches, almost concealing the nest. Little purple wildflowers have started to bloom and scatter the park floor like a warm blanket. *New life,* I think. *Will there ever be new life for me?* I don't believe so.

I feel Brent's fingers squeeze my hand lightly three times. My heart flutters, remembering that touch, three squeezes for *"I love you."* When I look over at him, he's staring at me, a strange, faraway look in his eyes. I think he squeezed my hand without even realizing it.

"Hey," he says, life returning to his face, "I bought a car. Want to see it?" He's up and off the swing, smiling as he tugs on my hand trying to get me to follow him.

"You did?" I ask, looking around. "Where is it?"

"In the parking lot. Come see?" he asks, his eyes pleading with me. He still has a goofy grin on his face and I can't resist.

"Okay." I laugh, his good mood contagious. "But I only have a few minutes."

"Oh yeah," he says, "curfew, right?"

I give him a cold look, warning him to drop it.

"Okay," he says. He takes my hand and holds it as we walk, looking over to smile at me every few steps. My heart races each time our eyes meet.

We walk on the path that lines the park, past the soccer field where a couple of boys have started passing a ball back and forth.

"So," I say, "did you meet any girls at college?"

"Yeah," he says, "I met a few girls."

I feel my lips curl into a frown. I kick at a rock on the path and send it tumbling in front of us.

"But don't worry," he says, leaning into me and whispering into my ear as we walk, "there's no one like you." He kisses my ear and holds his lips against it for just a moment as he inhales deeply before he pulls away.

I feel the heat rise to my face and I can't even look at him. I just keep looking forward as we walk. I'm so happy I feel like I could just float away. The heat expands between our hands and it sends a spark up my arm and a jolt through my heart, sending it into spasms. I inhale slowly, deeply, afraid I'm going to hyperventilate or pass out.

We stop at the edge of the path, where it meets the parking lot. There are three cars, two shiny new cars and a beat-up, rusted old blue car.

"That's it," he says, pointing at the beater. His smile reaches right across his face, and his eyes are glistening with happiness. "Isn't it great?" he says. "I worked part-time flipping burgers while at school and saved every penny. I bought it with my own money."

I feel a drop of rain splatter on the top of my head, then another on my cheek. I look up; the sky has darkened and is full of fat, dark clouds, threatening to burst.

"It's awesome," I say, truly thrilled to see him so happy.

"You know what this means, right?" he says, turning to me.

"What?" I ask.

He leans toward me and kisses me softly on the lips. He wraps his arms around me and holds me, burying his face into my neck. "I can take you away now. Anywhere you want to go," he whispers into my ear.

Without actually saying the words, he has finally brought up the topic that hovered over us, unspoken in the park just moments before.

"Oh, Brent." I sigh. "I can't." I pull away, out of his embrace and turn to walk away.

"Wait," he says, putting his hands on my shoulders. I stop. "I didn't mean to upset you. I only meant—" He drops his hands and I turn to him. "I mean, I thought . . ." he stammers, "I hoped we could finally be together. I have my own car now—we can run away together. I can keep you safe."

I smile as I feel my heart break again, looking into his sad face, still so hopeful, still full of belief that there is a better life out there for me. He doesn't understand. I have a promise to keep, no matter the cost.

I smile and hold back my tears. "That's sweet," I say. "You're sweet." I take both his hands into mine and kiss his fists. "You're the only person that's ever cared about me." I sigh.

"So then let's do it," he says.

"You have to go back to school," I say.

"Who cares about school," he says. "I was miserable. All I did was think about you and hate myself for leaving you behind."

"You had no choice. It was my choice to stay and it still is. I have to protect Elly."

More raindrops fall.

"So then let's go find her," he urges. "Let's go, right now."

"It won't be enough," I say. "Benson knows where she is. He will find her first and then it will all be for nothing. I can't. I'm sorry." I'm crying now; I feel the tears escape from my eyes and cover my cheeks, mixing with the raindrops that are coming down faster, landing on my head and my face. I wipe my eyes with my arm and will myself to stop crying. I have to be strong. I have to always be strong.

"Please," he begs. "I can't stand knowing you are still living with that monster. Doesn't your mother stop him?"

"It's complicated," I say. "My mom's sick. She can't help me. No one can. I have to go now, I have to be home soon." I pull away from him again.

"Wait," he says. "At least let me give you a ride. It's raining." He looks up at the dark clouds. "There's supposed to be a storm tonight."

We stand frozen, locked in a momentary stand-off in the parking lot. People have piled into the other two cars and they are backing out of the parking lot. There's no way I can make it home without getting soaked.

When I was little, I used to love thunderstorms. I would sit in the window with Mom and Dad and watch the lightning. Elly always slept through the storms. We'd each guess how many seconds there would be between each beautiful flash of light and then do a countdown together. The winner would do a little victory dance each time. Daddy's dancing always made me giggle. The next morning, we would go outside and splash through the puddles left by the storm.

I remember the first thunderstorm after Dad left. Benson had already moved in. Mom didn't want to watch the lightning storm with me so I was in bed, counting out the seconds between thunderclaps since I couldn't see the lightning flashes. It wasn't fun without Mom and Dad there. It was even a little scary. Benson came in and asked if we were okay. Elly didn't answer; she could sleep through anything. I had shaken my head from behind my blanket which was pulled up over my nose. "Do you want me to lie down with you?" he had asked. I nodded, so he came over and crawled under the blankets with me. At first, I felt safe again. In the dark it was almost like my dad had come back to us. But then Benson had shifted and put his hand on my thigh and underneath my nightgown. I tried to move away, but he held me close and said to be quiet, so we didn't wake up Elly. I remember staying completely still, like I was a statue, while my heart pounded so hard I thought it was going to jump right out of my chest.

I didn't even hear the lightning anymore. When he was finished, he moved back up beside me and whispered into my ear. "I only did that because you asked me to." I remember looking at him with wide eyes, shaking my head. "You wanted me to lie down with you, right?" he asked.

I nodded, because I had wanted him to. "See," he had said, "so you asked me to do this. You can't tell your mother, or she'll be mad at you and she'll leave you, just like your father did. He left because you were bad. You don't want her to leave, too, do you?" I shook my head quickly. "So then you better never tell her," he said and left our room, leaving me in the pitch black. I had been terrified that Mom would leave, too, so I hadn't said a word. I had even managed to convince myself that nothing had ever happened. That is, until Benson had slithered like a snake into my bed a second time, on the very same night they had told us that they had gotten married and that we had to start calling Benson "Daddy."

I don't want to walk home alone in the storm, I realize, trying to shake off the gross feeling that has come over me. I feel like thousands of little bugs are crawling all over my skin and I twitch, trying to knock them off me. *What harm could there be in letting Brent drive me home just this one time?*

"Okay," I say, "but just this once. For old time's sake."

He smiles and pulls me by the arm toward his car as the raindrops quicken. He opens the passenger door and helps me inside. "*Madame,*" he says, lifting my legs and placing them on the floor of the car.

I can't help but laugh as he closes the door and races around the car. By the time he jumps inside, the rain is shooting down like pellets and the sky is starting to rumble, sending out a warning of the storm to follow.

Brent wipes the rain from his face and starts the car. The engine roars to life and he pulls out of the parking lot.

The wipers swish furiously as we drive, but it's still hard to see. I look down at my watch, worried I'm already late and Benson will be mad, but Brent looks relaxed and happy for the excuse to drive extra slowly. He looks over at me and smiles every few seconds.

When he places his hand on my thigh, I don't flinch, but let it rest there, feeling the warmth from his hand radiate through me. I feel like we've driven down the road like this together a million times before. In another life I know we could live happily ever after.

"Let me out here," I say when we get around the corner from my house. "I'll walk the rest of the way."

"Don't be silly," he says. "It's pouring rain. I'll just pull up to your driveway."

"No, really," I argue, "here is fine. I don't mind the rain."

He ignores me and continues along as a feeling of dread rises in my chest. I try to ignore it, telling myself that I'm just being paranoid, but the feeling morphs into a sense of premonition. My stomach knots, the street lights start to blur, and it feels like the car is spinning uncontrollably down the road. *I need to keep Brent away from the madhouse that I call home.*

By the time he pulls into the driveway and stops just behind Benson's car, I feel like my heart is going to explode. I peer through the windshield to see if Benson is looking out any window. When I don't see his face, I relax, just slightly, and take a deep breath.

"Thanks for the ride," I say. "It was really good to see you today. But we shouldn't make a habit of it." *For your own good,* I think.

"Shh," he says, placing his finger across my lips. "It was good to see you, too, Danica," he whispers and leans in, kissing me softly on the lips.

I pull the door handle and practically throw myself outside, using every ounce of willpower I have to walk away from him.

I turn and wave goodbye, then change my wave to a shooing motion, urging him to drive away. He ignores me and waves at me, still smiling like a goofy schoolboy.

I turn and run the last few steps to the door, opening it quickly and slipping through, hoping that will get Brent to finally drive away. I stand, my back resting on the closed door as I shake the rain from my hair. Benson is not waiting for me, so I let out a breath of relief. *He still loves me,* I think happily, smiling at the thought of Brent's lips against mine.

"You're late," Benson's loud voice booms, jarring me from one of the few happy memories I have.

"Ah!" I shout, startled. "You scared me."

"What are you so happy about?" he asks. "You're late. Get upstairs, there's someone waiting for you."

"I just got in," I complain, "give me a sec." I start to peel off my wet jacket when I feel his hand against my face, knocking me away from the door.

Just as I'm regaining my balance, the front door flies open and Brent rushes past me, hands balled into fists. He takes a swing at Benson and connects with his nose. Benson stumbles back as blood erupts from his nose. Then he laughs, a wicked, evil laugh as the blood trickles into his mouth, turning his teeth red. He spits and his blood-filled saliva splats against the floor.

The next two minutes elapse in slow motion and I see every punch that Benson throws at Brent. I see every drop of blood that bursts from Brent's skin in response to the beating that Benson delivers. I hear every crack of bones as Benson throws Brent to the ground and stomps on his ribs.

I'm screaming, throwing my fists into Benson's back, begging him to stop. He just laughs and pushes me away. I fall to the floor, hitting my head on the ground.

I look up and see Benson dragging Brent by the collar out the front door. I force myself to my feet and follow them. At his car, Benson opens the driver door and throws Brent inside. Then he starts kicking the side of the car. He raises his leg and repeatedly kicks against the window, until glass explodes and shatters everywhere.

Thunder rumbles through the sky and a flash of lightning lights up the sky in the distance.

Benson goes to his own car and pulls out a baseball bat from the backseat and starts smashing it against the hood of Brent's car, against the windshield and across the top of the car. By the time he finishes his assault, the car is as beat up as Brent.

"You're getting off lucky this time, kid," he says. "Next time you step into my house, you're dead."

He drops the bat and saunters away from the car like he's on a leisurely Sunday stroll. When he passes me, he grabs my hair and pulls me behind him.

I look back toward the car as Benson drags me by the hair. Through the cracked windshield I see Brent pull himself up.

There is another flash of lightning as our eyes lock. His right eye is swollen, and his face is covered almost entirely in blood.

We continue staring at each other, lost in a world of pain, until Benson opens the front door and shoves me inside.

CHAPTER 12

Elaina

"We have to go, Laney," Dad shouts from the bottom of the stairs.

I spit out the toothpaste and lower my head to the tap to take in a gulp of water. I spit again and look into the mirror, into the reflection of my own eyes. *Who is Annie? Who is Rebecca? Think. Remember,* I command. Nothing comes to me. Frustrated, I smack my reflection and growl.

Max, who had been lying across my feet as I brushed my teeth, jumps up. He circles my legs and whines.

"Hurry up, or we're going to be late," Dad shouts. His voice is getting closer; he's coming up the stairs.

"I'm coming, hold your horses," I grumble and leave the bathroom. I pull my hair up into a ponytail as I run down the stairs. I meet him part way and push past him on my way to the bottom.

"Slow down," he complains as he bounces off the wall and grabs the railing.

"Speed up or slow down? Which is it?" I snarl at him. *Why hasn't he ever told me about Annie? Or Rebecca? Why hasn't he ever taken me to her grave? Where was her grave? Why were the flowers in the forest instead of in the cemetery? Was Annie dead, too? Why do*

I remember seeing his face at the park, all those years ago? So many questions and not a single answer.

Max follows me and pushes his nose into me as I bend down to pull on my sneakers. I give him a quick scratch behind his ear then pick up his ball and chuck it across the room. He turns and chases it, his nails scratching and slipping on the hardwood. I grab a jacket and hold it over my head to block the rain as I run out the door.

I'm sitting, buckled up, in the passenger seat of the car by the time Dad climbs into the passenger seat beside me. He's smiling like he doesn't have a care in the world.

"And we're off," he says in a cheery voice as he makes an exaggerated move to start the car and pretends to be surprised when the car roars to life. It was cute when I was five. Now it is just annoying.

He turns a knob and the windshield wipers come to life.

I roll my eyes at him and pull out my earphones, cranking the volume up high on my iPhone. A bouncy '80s dance song blares in my ears. I always play dance music whenever I need an instant pick-me-up. Even that's not working today.

"Are you looking forward to the summer?" he asks as we start driving away from our house. *Rebecca's house, not my house,* I think.

"Nope."

"How is Norman? He hasn't been around the house lately. Is everything okay with you two?"

"Yep."

"Do you want to take those headphones out so you can actually have a real conversation with me?" he asks.

"Nope."

I close my eyes and sink down into my seat. The seat warmer is on and it's starting to warm up my back. *How do I get him to tell me the truth?* I wonder.

I picture myself in the park, with Norman, that day when I nearly lost my marbles. He was so good. He had rubbed my back and told me everything was going to be okay as I twirled around looking for a ghost who was speaking to me. *Who was the girl on the slide with me? Annie? Rebecca? Why was she with me? Why did she push me toward Daddy and tell me I'd be safe? Was it a memory? Was it a dream? Am I going completely crazy?*

"Argh!" I yell and smack my hands on the dashboard.

Dad jumps in his seat beside me and slams on the brakes. I jolt forward and have to put both hands on the dash to brace myself. There's a loud squeal from behind us, then a honking sound. A car pulls up beside us. The driver's yelling at us through his closed window and flips Dad the bird. I lift my hand and flip the bird right back at the driver. My lips curl slightly upwards when I see a look of surprise register on his face. I see his lips move some more and I'm pretty sure he's swearing at me.

"Elaina, seriously," Dad says, putting his hand over mine and forcing my hand down. "Don't do that."

Dad slows down and the car squeals ahead of us. The driver pulls back into our lane, just barely missing our car with his back end.

Dad hits the brakes again.

I pull one earphone out and let it dangle, but I leave the other in. The music is still blaring. My happy song is still not working.

"Elaina Dawn Samson," Dad says sternly as he takes his foot off the brake and starts accelerating again.

Hearing him say my full name reminds me of the name change certificate tucked away in my bottom drawer. *Am I just a replacement?*

"What are you doing? You almost caused an accident," he complains.

"Whatever." I shrug.

"Don't just say 'whatever,' that was serious. Don't do that again. If you're angry about something, there are better ways to deal with your frustration."

I'm in no mood for his mumbo jumbo right now.

"So," he says. "What are you angry about?"

"Why do I have to go to this stupid thing anyway?" I ask.

"It's a Family Fun Day at my boss's cottage. All the employees are going with their families. Lower your volume," he says, "you're going to damage your eardrums."

"It's pissing out," I say, gesturing to the windshield as if he's blind to the blades working frantically to remove the water pounding against the windshield. "How much fun can we have at a cottage when it's pissing out?" I turn my volume up. I move my head in rhythm with the music.

He sighs and shakes his head. "Language," he says.

I roll my eyes.

"Are we all just supposed to stand around all day and get soaking wet? Or better yet, maybe we can all squeeze into his little cottage and sit there melting in the heat while everyone starts to sweat and stink."

"There will be waterskiing, kayaking, badminton, swimming. Rain or shine, there will be lots to do," he says.

"Sounds boring," I say.

"You enjoyed it last year," Dad counters. "And the year before that and the year before that," he continues.

"That was then," I say. "Things are different now."

"What's so different now?" he asks.

"Stuff," I mumble.

"That's helpful."

"I'm not a little kid anymore."

"You're sure acting like one," he says.

"Whatever."

"You can still have fun. Just because you're not a little girl anymore doesn't mean you have to stop having fun."

"What was I like when I was a baby?" I ask, changing the topic.

I've rattled him again. I can tell. He slows for a stop sign and takes his time looking both ways before he pulls into the intersection.

"You were a wonderful little girl," he finally says.

"No, I mean when I was a baby. Like right after I was born. Did I cry a lot? Did I keep you and Mom up all night or was I a good sleeper? What was I like?"

"You were . . ." he starts, then pauses, keeping his eyes on the road. "You were a great baby," he finally says.

"Bullshit," I grumble.

"Language, Elaina."

"This is stupid. I don't want to go to this thing today and I don't want to be stuck in a car with you."

"It will be fun. All the employees are going and taking their families."

"Are you sure I should be going then?" The words pop out before I have made the conscious decision to speak them. Now that they have been spoken, I am ready to force a conversation. I am finally ready to learn the truth. I need to know the truth.

"What does that mean?" Dad asks. I feel the car start to go a little faster and I notice his grip tighten on the steering wheel. His knuckles are starting to turn white. We pass by a speed limit sign and I notice Dad's going about ten kilometres over the limit. I must have really rattled him; he never speeds.

"You tell me," I challenge.

"I don't have time for riddles, Laney." He sighs. "Please just tell me what's on your mind." I feel the car slow down again. He returns to following the speed limit as he regains his composure.

The rain continues to pour down on us. We drive through a puddle and the water splashes up beside my window.

"Nothing."

"Something's going on," he says. "You haven't been yourself lately."

"Who have I been?" I ask, looking over at him to watch his face.

"You know what I mean," he chides. "You're just acting differently."

"Hmm," I say. "Am I acting like Rebecca?"

I notice a slight look of surprise cross his face before he catches himself. It was just a slight twitch of his eyebrow. If I hadn't been watching him closely, I would have missed it.

"Rebecca Dawn Samson," I say her name slowly, with a pause between each part of her name. "Maybe I took her personality as well as her name."

"What are you talking about?" he asks. His voice catches. I hear the tone of his voice change. He's nervous. I'm on to something here.

"You're the one who needs to stop speaking in riddles, Dad," I say. "Should I even call you 'Dad'?"

"Of course, you should. What else would you call me?" He's over-pronouncing all of his words now, a clear sign he's getting angry and trying to control it.

"Who is Rebecca?"

He takes a deep breath, keeping his eyes on the road the entire time. "I've told you, sweetie," he says, "your mother was sick. She was confused. She didn't know what was real and what was not." His voice appears calm, but it sounds forced. *He's definitely hiding something.*

"Oh, really," I say. "Are you sure about that?"

"I'm sure, Laney. You know how sick Mom was, you saw how confused she was. I know she scared you, especially in the end at the hospital. It was hard for both of us. Maybe it's time to talk to someone about it. Why don't I make another appointment with Dr. Grenner for you?"

"Nice try!" I shout. "Don't make this about me." Tears threaten, but I refuse to give in to them. I push some buttons on my phone and pull up a picture.

"It's okay to be angry about Mom's death. I was angry, too, but it's time to . . ."

"Beloved Angel," I say, cutting him off. "Rebecca Dawn," I continue, reading the card from the picture on my phone. I push my phone in front of him to show him the picture of the bouquet by the tree.

He continues to face forward, but I see his eyes shift to look at my phone. Finally, he turns to me. "Where did you get that?" he hollers. He reaches over and tries to grab for my phone. His face is distorted in a weird, crazed look, like he's been momentarily possessed. I pull the phone away from him, but I'm too slow. He's gotten a hold of the top of the phone. He tugs on it, trying to pull it from my grip. I squeeze my hands around it and pull back on the phone, keeping it from him.

We pull back and forth, in a tug of war with my phone, until the car swerves onto the shoulder.

A car behind us honks and Dad turns the wheel to get us back on the road.

"Are you going to keep lying to me?" I shout at him. "Keep telling me that Mom was confused, that she didn't know what she was talking about? How long do you expect me to keep believing your bullshit?"

The tire catches the shoulder again and Dad jerks the wheel to the left. We both keep pulling on my phone as our bodies jiggle in our seats while the car swerves back and forth. A car behind us honks over and over.

He looks over at me and our eyes lock in a staring stand-off. I feel the car bounce as we move off the smooth pavement and swerve back onto the soft gravel shoulder.

"I remember," I tell him. "I remember the day in the park. You said you were going to take one of us. She pushed me toward you. You kidnapped me," I yell. "You kidnapped me!" I recall my vision, if that's what it was, of a girl pushing me toward a man, toward Daddy, and saying, "Take her." *I didn't know him before that. Did I?* "Was it to replace Rebecca after she died?"

Dad releases his grip on my phone and retakes the steering wheel. He looks stunned, like I've just slapped him. He twists hard to the left to correct the car's direction.

"Was that Annie I was with in the park? Was she my sister?"

I feel the tires catch, then slip as we hit a puddle. Suddenly the car becomes a projectile rocket, hurling us across our lane and straight into oncoming traffic.

Time slows and I see each minute movement clearly. Dad's eyebrows raise and his eyes widen, like they're going to pop right out of the sockets as he realizes he's no longer in control of the car. He's madly twisting the steering wheel back and forth, but it's not doing anything. His leg is bouncing up and down as he hits the brake and releases, hits the brake and releases.

The windshield wipers continue to swipe furiously across the glass. The rain is coming down so hard it's like someone is standing above us with a hose.

My phone falls off my lap and down to my feet. I leave it and place both hands against the dash as I look up and see a silver SUV—*a Honda,* I have time to think—headed straight toward us.

From my side view I see Dad stomp on the brakes again. He's still trying madly to control the car by turning the steering wheel. I look up and see the face of the driver headed toward us. A man, with long hair and a long scraggly beard. There's a woman in the seat beside him. They both have the same frantic look as Dad. The woman is waving her arms, her mouth open in what must be a scream. The man is making the same wild movements as Dad with the steering wheel.

In one last moment, I look over at Dad. He turns his head to me. "I'm sorry," he says, jerking the steering wheel one last time. I feel the tires catch and the car swerves in response. Those are the last words he speaks to me before everything goes black.

CHAPTER 13

Danica

I'm sitting in my room when I hear tires squeal outside. I run to the window and watch Benson peel out of the driveway. He almost hits our neighbour who is out walking her dog. Her little rat-sized dog yips and jumps as it just misses being flattened into a pancake. Our neighbour balls her fist and swings her arm in the air at Benson. He just laughs at her and speeds off. The neighbours must love us; it's no wonder the houses on either side of us are put up for sale just about every year.

The branches on the tree outside my window are covered with a layer of ice. Snowflakes start to fall from the sky. They are small at first, but they get fatter and heavier as I sit in my window and watch them dance their way to the ground. I look down at the driveway below, picturing my body crumpled and bloodied from the impact. *If it were only myself that I was concerned about, I could easily jump,* I think. I'm not sure that I'm up high enough to get the desired result, but I'd happily try.

But there's someone else, someone more important that I am living for.

I sigh and leave the window.

I realize I'm thirsty, so I go downstairs. I stop in front of the couch. My mother is passed out, her mouth gaping open and drool dripping down her cheek. *Typical.*

"Where'd Benson go?" I ask her.

She doesn't move so I shake her shoulders. "Where'd he go?" I ask. Still nothing. "How long's he going to be gone?" I shake her harder and slap her face lightly. I have to force myself to keep the slaps light. I want to pull my hand way back and take a good swing at her. "Mom, where'd he go?" I ask again. I stare at her and laugh as I think about the word "Mom." She hasn't deserved the honour of that name in a long time.

Do I have time to do some snooping? That's really what I want to know.

She's useless, so I give up. I grab her bottle of vodka and take a drink. As the liquid slips down my throat I'm disappointed that it doesn't burn like it used to when I first tried it. Looking down at her, out cold, not a care in the world, I decide she's got it pretty easy. A few pills, a little bit of alcohol and she sleeps as soundly as a baby, not a care in the world. I grab her bottle of pills from the coffee table, pop the lid and dump one into my hand. *Time to join her in her alcohol- and pill-induced coma,* I decide. *Maybe it'll help me forget a few of my own problems, too.*

I flush the pill down with another swig of vodka then put the bottle and pills back on the coffee table. They must always be within arm's reach of the couch so that Crystal or Benson can keep her medicated with little effort. Heaven forbid she should have one conscious moment to think about the lives of the two little girls that she's completely messed up.

I realize that as much as I sometimes hate my father for abandoning us, I hate my mother more for what she's done.

I resist the urge to spit on her and go to the kitchen to dig around. I look through drawers and in the cupboard above the fridge. I grab two beers from the fridge and go upstairs. I decide to take a chance and look quickly through her room. I don't expect to find anything good, but I'm bored and need something to do. I run to my bedroom window and look outside to make sure the driveway is still empty then run back to her room.

I open the side table drawers and move things around. Pill bottles—some empty, some still full of pills—roll around in the drawer. I kneel and look under the bed. I go through all her dresser drawers, even pulling each one out to see if there is anything taped underneath. No luck. In her closet I shuffle clothes around. I find a wad of cash rolled up and tucked in a shoe. I pull out a few twenties, stuff them in my pocket and put the roll back.

There's a small box on the top shelf. I pull it down and pull everything out. It's just her old clothes. I'm about to give up and shove everything back in when I feel something hard move at the bottom. I grab and pull it out. It's a photo album. I flip open the cover and there's a picture of me, Elly, Mom and Dad.

My heartbeat immediately quickens. I close the cover and throw her clothes back in the box then replace it on the shelf. I grab the album and beer and run to my room. I open my window, so that I will hear Benson when he gets home. Then I pop the top off the first beer and hold on to the cap, flipping it around in my hand as I chug it down until the entire bottle is gone.

I'm happy I took the pill. I'm pretty sure I'm going to want to fall into the same comatose state as my mother once I'm done looking through the album.

I sit, cross-legged on the floor and open the album. I stare at the picture of the four of us for the longest time. Elly's a baby, maybe one year old. That would make me about three. We are lying in a pile, Mom and Dad on the floor, side by side, looking at the camera. I'm holding Elly on Mom's back and I'm sitting on Dad's. We're all smiling so big we had to have been laughing. Real happy laughing. We looked like a real family. Dad looks happy. I smile as I touch the picture, tracing his smile with my finger. In my other hand I'm still rolling the beer cap around and around my palm.

I must have done something really bad to make him leave us.

I turn the page quickly when I realize my smile has turned into a pout and I'm dripping tears onto the picture. I flip through each page, examine every photograph, trying to find some clue that shows when things went bad. I see Elly's face, over and over. We are together in every picture. We did everything together.

I remember how much I loved her, how much I still love her and miss her. Even with all the pain I've had to endure, I'd take ten times more pain to ensure she's safe and happy. I remember the day they brought her home from the hospital. I was waiting anxiously at home with our neighbour, a little old lady who I thought of as my grandmother. As soon as Mom walked in, carrying Elly, I rushed up to her and tried to jump up to see "my baby." Dad helped me sit on the couch and showed me where to put my arms as Mom lowered her onto my lap. I kissed her head and knew that I would never love anyone as much as I loved her. I was a big sister now, Dad had told me, and that came with a lot of responsibility. It was my job to protect her. I knew that being her big sister was the only thing I ever wanted to be in my whole life.

I pull a picture of Elly from the album and hold it to my chest. Instead of pushing the pain away like I usually do, I let myself feel it for once, really feel it. I allow the pain of her absence to burrow into my soul. I feel my heart shatter into a thousand pieces, shooting bits of heartache throughout my body, down my legs, through my arms, up into my brain. I cry. I'm broken. Without her I will never be whole again.

There's a pressure building up inside me, like I'm a hot kettle, my blood boiling intensely inside me, pushing to escape. I need to release the steam, but I can't. The tears pouring from my eyes are not enough. I feel my ears start to burn. My head pounds, my temples throb. It feels like I'm going explode. My breathing is shallow; it hurts if I try to take a deep breath, so I stick to short, fast breaths. I'm starting to feel dizzy. Everything hurts. I feel the loss of my sister in every single cell of my body. I can't take it anymore. I wish for an end, an end to my pain, my heartache, my life without Elly.

Ouch, I think. I twitch slightly in response to a jolt of pain in my palm. I've squeezed the bottle cap so tight in my fist that its sharp edge has cut into my skin. I open my hand and watch a fat drop of blood escape. I hold my hand sideways and watch as the blood trickles down my hand and falls to the floor. *The steam is escaping,* I think. The pounding lessens, just slightly.

I kick off my pants and sit back on the floor in my underwear. I take the bottle cap and scrape it against my thigh. I don't dig hard enough, so it just leaves a scratch on my skin. It's not enough. I do it again, making sure one of the pointy tips is right against my skin and I dig deep while I drag it across my thigh. I wince in response to the pain, but I feel the pressure release again and it is such a relief that I don't even feel the pain from the cut anymore. I do it again and again. Dragging, digging, cutting into my thigh. Then I lean back against my bed and take a deep breath. I feel my heart rate slowly return to normal. My temples stop throbbing. The pressure lessens.

I open my eyes and feel normal again. My leg is stinging. It's a mangled mess of blood and skin. The blood has already started to scab. I did make quite a mess, but it's such a relief to have let the pressure escape that I don't even care.

I hear Benson's car pull into the driveway, so I return the picture to the album and stuff it under my dresser, then run to the bathroom, wet a washcloth and wipe the blood away.

Next time I'll use a razor, I think. *I'll be able to cut deeper.*

I wake in the middle of the night, surprised that I'd fallen asleep and hadn't been woken up by Benson or some other freak. I lie still in bed, listening for footsteps. I'm so used to them now that they don't always wake me up to give me a few seconds' warning like they used to. My eyes adjust to the bit of light coming into my room from the street lights and the moon. I can see the outline of the top bunk above me. *Elly's bed.*

It's been so long since I slept in this room with her tucked in above me. I picture her up there, laughing as I tickled her and tucked her in each night. *I had to keep her safe,* I think. He would have gone after her next. *He did go after her,* I remember, a shudder running through me and causing goosebumps to erupt on the back of my neck.

There had been another party. There were a lot of parties after Benson moved in. I had tucked Elly in as usual and she went right to sleep like I told her to. I had lain awake, listening, waiting for the sound of footsteps to start down the hall. I knew they would come. The longer I waited, the sicker I felt. I jumped at every sound, the house shifting in the wind, a branch scratching against our window, a creak in the floor outside my door.

I heard lots of laughing and bottles clinking from the party. I thought Benson would be really drunk. Sometimes, after a party, he would wobble and stumble when he walked to my bed. His breath always smelled like beer and he spoke funny, slurring his words. One time he fell onto my bed like that and started snoring. I didn't move for the longest time, afraid I would wake him up and remind him what he had come for. I had just pretended I was a statue and didn't move. Eventually, I had slowly slithered out of my bed and slept on the floor. In the morning he was gone.

Hoping that he would be getting that drunk again, I had decided to hide on him that night. I figured that if he was drunk enough, he would just give up right away if I wasn't in my bed. Maybe he would fall onto my bed and pass out again. I decided that I could sleep on the floor underneath my bed with Benson passed out above me if it meant that I could escape from him for just one night. So, I had rolled out of bed and slipped underneath it. It was wishful thinking. He had stumbled into our room, and I could tell from his footsteps that he had wobbled as he walked toward my bed, but he didn't fall into a drunken coma. Instead, he had moved around, whispering my name. I felt the bed move under his weight as he had shifted around, feeling all around the mattress.

Finally, the bed had creaked and jiggled as he climbed off. *Yes, I outsmarted him,* I had thought, smiling from my hiding spot.

Then the bed had started to move again. It was creaking as he climbed the ladder. *Elly.*

I had rolled quickly out from under the bed and saw him halfway up the ladder to where Elly lay peacefully on the top bunk.

"I'm down here," I had said. "I must have fallen out of bed and rolled under there in my sleep."

There was enough light from the street lamp that I could see his expression. He may have been drunk, but he wasn't drunk enough that night to buy my lame excuse. His face twisted, his nose twitched, then he snorted at me and took another step upwards.

He was going to teach me a lesson for hiding on him.

He took another step up the ladder.

"I'm ready," I said and climbed onto my mattress. I held my breath, hoping with everything I had that he would leave Elly alone.

He stood on the ladder for what felt like hours. Finally, when he started to move again, I almost cried with relief when I realized he was climbing back down the ladder.

When he had climbed into my bed, he had put his hand around my throat and whispered in my ear, "Pull that stunt again and Elly's mine. You got it?"

I had nodded quickly, gripped with terror at the realization that I would not be able to protect Elly from him forever.

I smile now, revelling in the twisted pleasure of knowing that I had been wrong. I had found a way to protect Elly from him forever. As long as I did what he said, she would always be safe from him.

I get out of bed and open my door a crack to listen. It's quiet and dark. Only a faint light glows softly from the kitchen. I tiptoe down the stairs. Mom is asleep on one couch, and Benson is snoring loudly on the other. There is a pile of empty beer bottles on the floor beside him. *My lucky night,* I think. *He got too drunk to even attempt to come upstairs. If only I could be so lucky every night.*

I see an outline of something else on the floor, so I step closer to look. I knock the empties aside and pick it up.

It's a gun.

I turn it over in my hands, looking at it. My hands start to tremble with excitement.

I take it in my right hand, hold it, squeezing the handle with my whole fist. I don't trust myself enough to rest my finger on the trigger. I take a step toward the couch. I'm standing over Benson now. I raise the gun, holding it now with two hands trying to keep it steady. I aim it at his face and stand there, watching him snore. I remember the first night he crawled into my bed. I think about every night he's crawled into my bed since. I picture him on the ladder, crawling toward Elly.

Then I picture myself pulling the trigger, blowing a hole in his face. I see his head burst like a water balloon, spreading his brains across the couch. It would solve all my problems. Elly would be free. I would be free.

I think about how much he's hurt me. How much he's taken from me. My sister. My boyfriend. My mother. My self-respect. My future. I want to pay him back for all of it. I want to hurt him. I want to hear him cry out in pain and laugh as he suffers.

All I have to do is squeeze the trigger.

I keep watching him. He takes a deep breath in, snorts, chokes, then pushes the air out with a loud rumble. His eyes twitch beneath his lids. *What do monsters like him dream about?* I wonder.

I decide a bullet to the head is too easy on him. I shift, stepping to the side and point the gun at his groin instead. *I'll start here and let him suffer for a little while before I put him out of his misery.* For a moment, I'm startled by how happy the thought makes me. I feel a sense of relief wash over me. It feels like freedom, like I can finally be rid of the monster.

I'm going to pull the trigger.

I want to pull the trigger.

I will my finger to move, to find the trigger, to fire the gun.

I can't.

I reach with my left hand and try to pull my index finger off the handle, to move it to the trigger. I'm squeezing my right hand so tight that my finger doesn't budge.

Do it! I command, but I just stand there, frozen.

Disgusted and angry with myself, I lower the gun and put it back on the floor. I knock an empty bottle and it clinks as it rolls and bumps into another empty. I berate myself before I turn and run back up the stairs, two at a time and throw myself down on my bed. I bury my face in my pillow and scream, kicking my feet and smacking my arms against my bed.

Why couldn't I pull the trigger?

CHAPTER 14

Elaina

I push open the door, walk in, and lie down on the burgundy couch. It's just as comfortable as I remember. As I stretch out my legs and cup my hands behind my head, I close my eyes and think, *It's official, I am crazy.*

"Hello, Laney," Dr. Grenner says, walking from her desk to the chair across from me. "It's been a while. How are you?" She adjusts her skirt as she sinks into the chair.

"I'm lying down." I force a laugh out. "Doesn't that answer your question? I think it's time to lock me up and throw away the key."

The sun is shining through one of the windows, right into my eyes. I squint and shield my eyes with my hand as I try to look at her. The beautiful, bright summer day is a complete contrast to how I feel inside. The songs from the birds chirping happily outside make me angry. I wish I had some rocks to throw at them to shut them up and chase them away. I want everyone and everything to feel as miserable as I do.

"I'm sorry," she says, getting back up. "Let me close the blinds." She walks over to the windows, pulls a string to let the blinds down and closes the curtains over top. Aside from a little lamp on her desk, which has a very dim light bulb, the room is now dark. I feel my heart start to race. I look over to the door, watching it to see if it opens, waiting for the monster to come for me here. I twist the cuff of my shirt between my fingers.

"It's dark," I manage to mumble. "The monster comes when it's dark." My eyes are darting around the room. *Will it come through the door or is it already in here, just waiting for the lights to go out?*

I can hear the monster breathing, quick, noisy breaths. I lean over and look under the couch. I'm starting to feel dizzy, so I draw in a long, deep breath. I close my eyes and whisper, "Go away, monster."

"Would you like me to turn on some more lights?" Dr. Grenner asks.

I turn my head quickly toward her voice and nod. I'm on high alert; I know the monster is coming for me. I follow her with my eyes as she flips the light switch and the bright light on the ceiling turns on. As my eyes adjust to the brighter light, I feel myself start to calm down. *I'm safe now.* I let out a sigh of relief.

"Is the monster here?" she asks.

I shake my head.

"Have you seen the monster before?"

I look around the room one more time to make sure it's not coming for me, then I look at her and nod.

"What does it look like?"

I close my eyes. I don't want to remember the monster, but an image of it pops in my head. It makes my stomach knot and my hands feel sweaty as I twist them together. I lift my right thumb to my mouth and chew on the nail as I speak.

"It's big," I say, sinking into the couch as if it could protect me. "It's tall." I saw its shadow against the wall so many times. But I only ever saw its face once. That one time was enough to haunt my dreams for the rest of my life. "It has long, stringy hair. Big, crooked teeth. Big creepy eyes." I remember seeing it, peering at me from over the railing of my bunk bed. I was so scared I thought I was going to die.

"It's not in here now," she says.

I look around the room. "Are you sure?"

"I'm sure, Laney."

I squeeze my eyes shut and sing the monster song in my head, just in case.

"Do you need a minute?" she asks.

I shake my head. "I don't like the dark."

"Is that something new?" she asks.

I shake my head again. "I sleep with a light on. I have for as long as I can remember," I say.

"Does it make you feel safe to have a light on?"

I nod.

"That's good," she says. "It's good to do things, to have strategies to help yourself feel safe." She smiles at me.

I lower my head and look at my feet propped up on the couch. I feel like a two-year-old needing to sleep with a night light.

"I heard about the accident," she says, changing subjects. "Your injuries are healing nicely," she adds, looking closely at me, like she's studying my face.

Can she tell how crazy I am just by looking at me? I wonder.

I put my hand up to my face and rub a scar above my right eye. The stitches have dissolved, and my skin feels bumpy beneath my touch. "Yeah, I was lucky. Dad was able to swerve the car enough so that we didn't hit head on. The car hit us on the side instead." I close my eyes and relive the last moment before the car exploded around me and my world went black.

"On the driver's side," Dr. Grenner prods. She's looking down at her clipboard. She already knows the answer. Dad must have told her when he booked the appointment for me.

"Yes."

"It sounds like you were lucky," she says.

I feel guilty.

"How do you feel about that?"

What? Can she read my mind?

"How do you feel about that?" she repeats.

"Fine," I lie.

I look up at her. She's staring at me. Not in a weird or creepy kind of way, but like she's trying to draw the truth from me. *I can't tell her.*

"I'm fine about it. Whatever," I say.

"Your father saved you by swerving the way he did, didn't he?"

"I guess."

"What happened to the people in the other vehicle?" she asks.

I twist my hands together; I see their faces. I see the fear in their eyes, I feel it in my heart.

"Were they hurt?" she asks.

I nod slightly.

"But they will be okay?" she prods.

I nod again. My body shakes slightly as I cry. I shift my body on the couch; it's getting hot. I'm starting to feel sweaty in the warm, cozy couch. I kick off my shoes.

"And your father," she says. "He's going to be okay."

I nod. "He got smashed up. Broken nose, a few broken ribs and a broken arm. His brain was bleeding, he almost died, but the doctors saved him."

"And now you feeeellllll . . ." She exaggerates the last word, waiting for me to jump in. I stay silent.

"Guilty?" she asks.

I turn to her. *How does she know?* I start twisting my hands again, like I'm trying to wring out a sponge.

"It wasn't your fault," she comforts.

My body is shaking like crazy now. Tears are spilling from my eyes, soaking my cheeks, the way the rain soaked the windshield on the day of the accident.

"It was my fault," I whisper.

I see myself in the car, tugging on my phone as Dad tried to take it from me. I had taunted him with the words from the flower card. I was trying to start a fight with him. I wanted to force him to tell me who Rebecca was. Then I see myself in his hospital room. I see his body, bloody and broken on the bed. I remember the last words I spoke to him, *"You kidnapped me."*

Ridiculous.

Or was it?

"He'll keep you safe," the girl—*it had to have been Annie*—*had said to me when she pushed me toward the man in the park, toward my father.*

"He kept me safe," I say out loud. "He kept me safe, just like she said he would." I look at Dr. Grenner. I notice that she's watching me, but her face fades away from my consciousness and I'm back in the hospital, standing over Daddy's bloody, broken body.

"Even after I accused him of—of—" *Kidnap, I can't say that word out loud.* "He still kept me safe. He swerved the car so that he took the direct impact away from me. The policeman said if we had hit head on, I would have been killed. By swerving the way he did I escaped with just a few scratches, but he almost died. The doctors said he should have died. It was a miracle that he lived."

I'm back in the hospital with him, holding his hand while he's sleeping. He's been asleep since the accident. Doctors and nurses keep coming and going. They read his chart, push a few buttons on the machines, pump some medicine into him, then disappear again. "Wake up, Daddy," I cry. "Please wake up," I beg and squeeze his hand. "I'm sorry about Rebecca. I don't care if I'm just her replacement. You don't have to tell me anything about her. Just please wake up, Daddy."

I'm vaguely aware of Dr. Grenner's gaze upon me. But I stay, lost in my memory, lost in the knowledge that Daddy has always kept me safe. *Safe from everything. Safe from the monsters. Monsters!*

I feel my heartbeat quicken. My head feels cool as beads of sweat start to form. My eyes move wildly beneath my closed lids. *The monsters are coming.* I reach for Bunny Boo. *He's not there. Oh no, what do I do now? My song. I start saying the words from my song.*

"Go away, monster, I'm not afraid of you," I whisper the words aloud. "I'll make you go away, I know what to do." My voice is getting louder, I'm starting to sing the words now. "I keep my eyes closed and sing my song. And when I wake up, you'll be . . ." I open my eyes and look around, frantic. "Gone!" I shout.

"Gone," I repeat. "She's gone! Where is she?" I scream at Dr. Grenner. I jump off the couch and run around her office. I look behind the giant flowerpot, I look under her desk, I look behind the couch. I'm wild with fear. *I'm possessed, I must be. I can't stop myself from looking even though I know she's not in this room.*

I run up to Dr. Grenner and grab her by the collar. I stare straight into her eyes. "Where is she?" I shout at her as I shake her. I think I'm spitting at her as I shout, but I can't stop. "Where is Annie?" I'm hysterical now. *I have to find her.* "Where is Annie?" I repeat, screaming the words in a strangled, tortured voice. "The monster's got her! The monster's got her!" I let go of Dr. Grenner's collar and drop to the floor. I curl up in the fetal position and start to rock myself.

I saw the monster's face. I was lying in bed, quiet and still, just as Annie had told me to do. The monster came in our room; I could see its shadow creeping along the wall. I felt the bed move when the monster climbed into Annie's bed. I heard its deep, raspy voice calling for her.

She wasn't there.

She was hiding from the monster.

I smiled. *She is so smart,* I had thought.

Then I felt the bed move some more. I saw the monster's face peer over the railing on my bed. *It was coming for me.*

I had squeezed my eyes shut, singing my song in my head. I tightened my arm on Bunny Boo. I didn't move. I had stayed completely still just like she told me to and kept singing the song. The monster kept moving closer.

Then it stopped.

I heard her voice.

"I'm down here," she said. "I'm ready."

The monster turned away from me. He went for her instead. I felt the bed move. I heard her cry.

She had led the monster away from me and I hadn't done anything to stop the monster from hurting her.

"I'm going crazy. I'm crazy," I repeat as I continue to rock myself at Dr. Grenner's feet.

"You're not crazy," she says, leaning down to rub my arm. It's no consolation. Her words don't mean anything. My mind is racing. *I've completely snapped.*

"Where is she? Where is Annie?" I'm choking the words out; my throat feels like it's closing up. "Where is she?"

"I'm sorry, Laney, I don't know where Annie is," Dr. Grenner says soothingly. She's trying to calm me down using the soft tone of her voice.

"I do," a voice says. I look up. *It's Daddy.* He's pushed the office door open and he's rushing toward me. He's moving fast, considering all of the broken bones that he has.

"I'm so sorry, Laney," he says. "I know where Annie is."

CHAPTER 15

Danica

B irds chirping in the tree outside my window wake me up. I pull the blanket over my head and try to drown them out. *So cheery and full of life,* I think. *I'd like to ping them off one by one with a sling shot.*

Why am I the only one meant to suffer? I wonder. Then I remember: *It's because I deserve to suffer. I was bad. I chased my father away from us. I'm the reason he left us. I'm the reason Mom was lonely and sad enough to let Benson into our lives. It's my fault Benson hurts me. Everything is my fault.*

I accept that I have to suffer. I'm just thankful that Elly didn't have to pay the price for my mistakes, too. *Or did she?* In order to be safe, I had to send her away with a stranger. She had to leave the only family she had ever known and start a new life with someone we had met in the park. *Who was he?*

I had seen him in the park so many times before that day. *But did that mean I knew him? Did that mean I could trust him with the person I treasured most in the world? He had promised he would keep her safe. As a five-year-old, I had trusted that promise. Almost fifteen years later, did I still trust it?*

Elly and I used to go to that park almost every day, and most days we went a couple times each day. We were always by ourselves; Mom was always too sick to take us and Benson just laughed and kicked me the first time I asked him to take us so I had never asked him again. After he had started coming into our room at night, I was happy he wouldn't take us. Part of the reason we spent so much time at the park was just to get away from him, away from his insults, shoves, and dirty looks.

That man was there almost every day, too. With a little girl about Elly's age. They laughed and had fun together. She always wore pretty dresses and sometimes had flowers in her hair. Sometimes they sat in the middle of the park and had a picnic, other times they scampered through the park and picked the wildflowers growing in the grass.

I remember wishing that he were our daddy, wishing that he would play with us and laugh with us like he did with the little girl. Wishing that we could sit on the blanket with him in the middle of the park and dig into the picnic basket to feast on the watermelon and apple slices and thick sandwiches filled with cheese and sliced meats, instead of just the peanut butter sandwiches I made for us most days.

Some days we went to the park just so I could look for them. When Benson was particularly mean, or Mom followed his lead and smacked us around, just for being there, we disappeared to the park with the hopes of seeing them, so I could dream about our other life, our better life, with this man as our father. We'd be happy and safe and cared for.

Other days we didn't go to the park because I felt so sad that I chased our own dad away. The days when I could remember that he loved us, that he had played with us like that man played with his daughter. Sometimes I could remember playing in that park with our dad, laughing and having fun with him and Elly, and with Mom, too. On those days when I could remember, I had to stay away from the park, no matter how much Elly begged me; I couldn't take us to the park those days, because it made my heart hurt to watch the life we should have had, that we could have had, if only I was a better daughter, if only I didn't make him want to leave us. It's my fault we didn't have a father, and I needed to be punished for that.

Then, one day, they weren't there. Then the next day they weren't there again. I remember looking for them, day after day. I had missed them. Aside from Elly, their joy and laughter had been the only happiness I had in my life.

Then one day the man had shown up in the park again. There was no joy on his face, no laughter in his voice, no little girl on his arm. *Where had she gone?* I wondered. He would sit on a bench, the same one every time, and watch us. Some days he grasped a handful of wildflowers from the park. He sat there so long that the flowers drooped in his hands and looked as sad as his face did.

It felt good, knowing he was there. It felt like he was protecting us, keeping us safe. One day, I caught him smiling as he watched us play. He had turned and looked away when he noticed me smiling back at him. I remember feeling happy that we made him smile again. *If he was my daddy I would never do anything bad again,* I told myself.

And then, that one morning, the last morning in the park, it was different. He hadn't been on his usual bench when we got to the park. I thought I saw him standing at the edge of the park so I had waved to him, but he hadn't waved back.

Then he was standing at the slide with us. He had looked nervous. He said he would take one of us with him. I got to choose. I wanted to tell him to pick me. I wanted to go with him so badly. I wanted to have picnics and pick wildflowers and play on the swing with him. I wanted to go home to a house without Benson, where I could sleep at night without listening for footsteps.

But I could never leave Elly alone with the monster. I knew he was the answer to my greatest wish. If he took Elly, she would be safe forever from Benson. But in order to make my greatest wish come true, I would have to give her up forever, too. I wouldn't be her big sister anymore. I wouldn't have anyone to play with in the park and to push on the swings.

I knew I would be okay. I knew I was strong enough to handle anything Benson did to me. I knew I could just close my eyes and pretend nothing was happening. But Elly was just a little girl, so sweet, so fragile. The monster would have killed her. I couldn't let that happen. I had to save her. I knew what I had to do.

So, I had given the man the only answer I could. "Take her," I had said and pushed Elly toward him. Elly had turned and looked at me with her big, brown eyes wide open. "He'll keep you safe," I whispered and kissed her cheek, "safe from the monsters."

She started to whimper.

"But you have to promise me something," I had said to the man, stepping toward him with my hands on my hips. I must have been so intimidating, all three feet of me.

"Anything," the man had said.

"You have to promise that you will keep her safe. That you will love her and protect her from the monster."

"I promise," he had said.

"Pinky swear?" I asked, holding my hand out to him.

He had linked his pinky in mine and nodded as our eyes locked.

"Cross my heart and hope to die," the man had said, making an X over his heart with his free hand. Then he took Elly's hand and walked her out of the park.

As she walked with him, she kept looking back at me. I felt a piece of myself get torn away with each step she took. Eventually, she stopped turning around and just looked straight ahead.

As I watched them walk out of the park, I remember picturing my heart jump out of my body and into hers so that she would take a piece of me with her. So that I could feel just a tiny bit of the happiness that she would have in her new life. So that I could return to the monster and be numb to the pain that he inflicted on me. I had known in that moment, that I would never be whole again, not until we were together again one day. I knew that day would come when the time was right.

"Danny," I hear Benson shout from downstairs.

I ignore him.

"Hurry up, Danny!" Benson shouts. "I don't have all day, you know."

"What do you want?" I ask, climbing out of bed and slamming my bedroom door behind me. I peer into my mom's room and there she is, passed out on the bed. *Useless witch,* I think and pull her door closed. I take the steps two at a time as I pull a tank top over my head. I trip on the last step and stumble, catching myself before I hit one of the end tables.

"Go get the mail," he says.

"Why can't you get it, just this once?" I ask. My head is foggy from the pills he gave me and I'm sore and tired from the latest "episode" we taped.

"I gotta get this online," he says, fiddling with his phone. "I got people paying me good money for this. I can't keep them waiting."

"But I'm tired and I'm sore," I say, rubbing my side. "Your friend bit me. Am I bleeding?" I ask, lifting my shirt and turning toward him.

"Suck it up," he says and kicks his foot out toward me. Luckily, I'm too far away so he just kicks the air. "Get out of here and get the mail. Now!" he shouts.

"Fine," I say and turn to dig the mailbox key out of a drawer. His wallet's sitting on top of the cabinet. I take a quick look behind me and see that he's preoccupied with his phone, so I turn my back to him again and shift to block his view. With one hand I shuffle around in the drawer, and with the other I pop open his wallet and grab a couple of twenties, then flip it closed before turning around again to lift up the mailbox key to show him. He doesn't even look up.

I grab a stale muffin from the counter; it already has a bite out of it, but I don't even care anymore. At least it's food. These days there is a serious lack of anything edible in the house.

I stuff my feet into my shoes.

His sickening laugh follows me out the door, until I slam it shut behind me. I stop, lean back against it and think—as I do at least once every single day—about killing myself. I could just step out in front of a car on my way to the mailbox. *Did cars even drive fast enough down this road to kill me?* I wonder as a car putters by, going no more than fifty. *I'd probably just get maimed and lose an arm or a leg. Benson probably knew people who would pay extra for that.*

As usual, there was only one thought that kept me from jumping out in front of the next car that passed. *Elly.*

At the mailbox I stick the key in and pull out the mail, flipping through it as I always did. Benson would freak if he knew I checked through his mail. That's why I did it. I always pulled at least one thing out, ripped it up and threw it away, usually a hydro bill or a Visa bill. Once, after I threw away four Visa bills in a row, I heard him on the phone screaming at someone, complaining that his latest online purchase didn't go through because his credit card was coming up as declined. I sat in my bedroom and laughed so hard I had tears rolling down my cheeks. He screamed at them for over half an hour before he slammed the phone down and went racing out of the house, his tires squealing in the driveway. That was my best work to date.

Hmm, I think, flipping through the usual boring mail. *What to throw away this time?* I stop, frozen in place, as I look at an envelope, our address written in small letters, with large capital letters written above it: ANNIE.

I drop everything in my hands except for that envelope. Only one person had ever called me Annie.

I rip it open and pull out a handwritten letter folded around a picture. I slide the picture out and stare at it, mesmerized by the girl staring back at me. *Elly!*

She looks perfect. And happy. And safe.

Tears erupt and burst from my eyes, soaking my cheeks. My body is shaking so much I almost can't flip the letter open. Suddenly everything in my life has been worth it. *I've kept Elly safe. I've been a good sister.* Nothing else matters.

I struggle with the envelope and finally rip it open.

> *Annie,*
>
> *I don't know if you still live at this address, but if you do, I hope this letter finds you well. First off, I want you to know that Elaina has grown into a wonderful young woman, someone you would be very proud of. In recent years she has started remembering you and she would like to see you. We moved far away so no one could ever find us, so if you have any interest in seeing her again, please call.*
>
> *Sincerely,*
>
> *George*

My hands shake as I read the number scrawled at the bottom of the letter. *Elly is safe! She wants to meet me? I can't,* I think, *I can't let her see what I've become. No.*

I read the letter again and again, staring at the picture of Elly that I'm holding beside it.

I reread the words in the letter: *No one could ever find us.*

Was that true? Had Benson's threats all these years been a bluff? Did he really know where she was?

CHAPTER 16

Elaina

Back home, Dad leads me to the couch. "Sit here," he says. I do as he says. I feel like I'm in a trance. *He knows where Annie is.*

He sits beside me and takes my hands in his. Max jumps up beside me and tucks his head under my arm.

"I'm so sorry, Laney," he starts, "I thought I was protecting you by keeping the truth from you. I thought you were too young to remember any of it."

I look at him. I can see the pain in his eyes. "It's a long story," he says. "Are you sure you're ready for it?"

I nod. I'm holding my breath and biting my lip, ready to hear whatever story he has to tell me. *Just tell me where she is!* I want to scream at him.

"Please," he says, "know that I love you dearly, not because you are a replacement for someone else, but because you are my daughter, you own a piece of my heart. Try not to judge me. I know I made mistakes, but I made them with the best of intentions."

I just stare at him.

He takes a deep breath in, then pushes it out loudly. "Okay," he says. "So I guess I'll start at the beginning?" He looks to me for confirmation.

I nod.

"Nancy and I started dating in high school," he starts. "We went to the same college and got married the day after graduation. We started trying for a family right away. We both wanted to have a lot of children. Seven years later, we still hadn't been lucky enough to become parents. Over the next four years, we tried every procedure there was. We spent every penny we had. Finally, after so many years of heartbreak, just when we had almost given up hope, we welcomed Rebecca into the world. We were scared the entire time Nancy carried her. We had lost one baby at birth, three more through miscarriages. We were terrified every single day of her pregnancy. When Rebecca came into the world hollering, Nancy and I cried. We finally had a child. It was the happiest day of our lives."

Dad squeezes my hands and I look up at him. He's staring off into space, like he's watching the movie of his life unfold before his eyes.

Max jumps up to lick my face and I rub his belly to get him to lie back down. I don't want him to disturb Dad from his trance-like state and risk him stopping his story.

"We brought her home from the hospital and doted on her. She made every struggle we had ever been through worth it. She was a delight. She was perfect. Nancy quit her job so that she could become a full-time mom. We had everything we ever wanted. When Rebecca was two, we bought a house in a new neighbourhood that had good schools, nice parks and friendly people. A nice, safe neighbourhood for her to grow up in. She loved to play on the swings, zip down the slide, run through the grass. She loved life. She was happy. I took her to the park nearly every day. That's where I first saw you and your sister. I noticed the two of you right away because you both looked so much like my Rebecca. I didn't pay much attention to you at first, but after I noticed the two of you were there on your own all the time, I started to worry about you. You looked about the same age as

Rebecca, and your sister, Annie, looked only a couple years older than you."

My stomach tightens; I know we are getting to a bad part.

"On the last morning of Rebecca's life, I was getting her ready to go to the park. But she wasn't feeling good, she didn't want to go. Nancy took her upstairs to give her a bath instead. She loved to play in the tub, and when she wasn't feeling good, it always made her feel better. I decided to go for a run. I enjoyed running and tried to go for a jog every day. I decided to do a longer run— since we weren't going to get to the park, I figured I had a little more time. So, I ran through the woods and by the water, and even stopped to take a break and watch the ducks play for a few minutes. When I got home, I could hear Nancy screaming before I even reached the door. I ran upstairs, Rebecca was lying on the bath mat and Nancy was doing CPR on her, screaming in between breaths. I ran to them. I took over for Nancy, desperate to breathe life back into our little angel.

Nancy stood over me, watching, rambling on and on. 'She wanted her rubber ducky,' she said. 'I only turned away for a second. What have I done? What have I done?' she repeated over and over."

Max comes shifts under my hand, reminding me not to slack off with the belly rubs.

"She was gone. Rebecca had died. There was nothing we could do to bring her back," he says. Some tears have escaped and are trickling down his cheek. "Nancy flipped out, I think she had a mental breakdown. I didn't know what to do. She stood up and started smacking her head against the glass mirror. 'I want to die, too,' she cried. 'I want to go with her.' My mind was racing, our little girl was gone. How would we go on? It had taken so long for us to have Rebecca. I knew we couldn't go through the pain and heartache of trying to have another baby. Then I had an idea. It was such a despicable idea that I couldn't even tell Nancy. But I had convinced her that we shouldn't tell anybody about Rebecca.

She was in such shock that she probably didn't understand what I was saying. We were still new enough in town that we hadn't made any friends. Nobody really knew us. Our neighbours were older and didn't ask questions. I wrapped Rebecca up in her favourite blanket and I took her for a drive. My family owns some property up north that's been in my family for years. It's all forest and swampland in the middle of nowhere. No one's ever wanted to build on it. I took Rebecca up there and buried her on a hill, beside a maple tree, so she would get shade in the summer and could watch the leaves turn colours in the fall. A really nice spot. She would have really liked it. Then I came home and we tried to live a life without Rebecca. Nancy couldn't deal with the grief and the guilt. She tried to kill herself three times by taking all her pills at once. I hid her pills, but she found them. She turned the house upside down looking for them. I had to start taking them with me to work. I started going home every day at lunch to check on her. Sometimes she would be so angry, she'd scream at me, hit me, beg me for her pills. Other days she would just be sitting in her chair staring out the window. Some days, the hardest ones to witness, she would sit in an empty bathtub, rock back and forth and cry Rebecca's name for hours."

I watch his face as he tells me the story. I squeeze his hand and feel my heart fill with love and sadness for him, for both of them. Another pang of guilt washes over me as I remember how little attention I gave to my mom her last few years. The more bedridden she became, and the more she rambled on with her crazy talk, the less time I had wanted to spend with her. Holed up in her bedroom, it was easy to forget about her as I went about my busy life. I hadn't even noticed the pain she was in. *She lost two daughters,* I realized sadly.

"I continued to run almost every day. It was the only thing that kept me sane. I saw you and your sister at the park, alone, so many times. I was so angry. Nancy and I would have given anything to have Rebecca back, to take care of her and look out for her, and your parents didn't seem to care. They just let two little girls go off alone with no one to protect them. It wasn't fair. Each time I saw you, I fought the urge to take both of you. I wanted to teach your parents a lesson. I wanted them to suffer and feel the pain of loss because I didn't think they deserved to be parents. I was so full of anger and hate I almost couldn't function anymore."

He pauses, closes his eyes and drops his chin to his chest. He stays like that for a few seconds, takes a few deep breaths and lets them out. Then he continues his story. "On that morning, I had woken up and Nancy was smiling for the first time since Rebecca's death. I had forgotten how beautiful she was when she smiled. She was in the kitchen, frying up some bacon. I didn't know what had happened. I didn't know what had changed. 'I'm going for a run,' I had said. 'Shh,' she had replied, still smiling as she walked over to me and kissed me on the cheek. 'Rebecca's still sleeping. Go for your run and when you get home—I'll wake her up to have breakfast with us.' She had turned back to the stove and continued cooking. I put on my shoes and ran straight to the park. Could I pull it off? I thought as I ran. If Nancy had lost touch with reality, maybe I could bring home just one of you and convince her it was Rebecca. Then your parents would still have one child left and I wouldn't be leaving them completely lost. I would be doing it out of love, not out of hate. By the time I got to the park I had convinced myself to leave it up to fate. If you were alone at the park, I would take one of you home with me and leave the other for your parents. A nice, fair arrangement where we each ended up with one child to care for. If you weren't there, it wasn't meant to be, and I would go home to my smiling wife and pretend child."

He pauses again and looks at me. His face is stuck between a smile and a frown. I squeeze his hand again and smile to let him know I'm still here, still listening to him.

"My heart was pounding so fast," he continues. "It was early in the morning and it was foggy. I was afraid you wouldn't be at the park alone on a morning like that, so I went the long way, around the park and through the forest. I stopped running before I got through the forest. I didn't know if I could take the heartbreak if you weren't there. I didn't know if I could go home empty-handed and be happy to just pretend Rebecca was there with us. So, I prayed, with each step I took closer to the edge of the forest I prayed that the two of you would be playing at the park alone. I promised myself that if you were, that if I was able to take one of you home to be my daughter, that I would be the best father there could ever be and that I would make up for anything you would miss from your current life. I promised that in order to honour the sacrifice that your parents were going to have to make in losing you, I would give you the happiest childhood possible. When I saw the playground through the opening of the trees, I stopped walking. I held my breath. In my heart, one of you had already become my daughter. I knew I couldn't go home alone. I continued to hold my breath as I took the last steps out of the forest. I almost cried when I saw you both playing on the swings. Your sister was pushing you as she always did. I was about to walk toward you when your sister waved at someone. I froze. I hadn't even thought about other people in the park. I panicked. What if someone saw? What if they came for you once I got you home? I couldn't live through another loss. Your sister waved at me, but I couldn't move. I had to be sure the park was empty. I had to be sure no one would see me. So I stood there and watched. When I was sure there was no one watching, I walked up to you."

"I remember that," I say. "I remember going down the slide and stopping at the bottom. Annie usually took off running at the bottom. But she stood still. I was afraid so I stood behind her and buried my face in her back. I heard her talking to someone, but I couldn't see who it was. Then I heard someone ask how old we were. I was excited—I had just turned three and Annie taught me how to hold up three fingers. Then Annie pulled me out from behind her and pushed me away from her. 'Take her,' she said. She whispered in my ear, 'You'll be okay. He'll keep you safe. I love you, Elly Belly, always remember that.' But I didn't remember that," I cry out, overcome with panic. "I forgot about her," I say. "I forgot all about her and left her alone with the monster. He's got her—I know he's got her. We have to save her." I stand up, pull on Dad's hand. "You have to help me save her. We have to find her." I'm looking around the living room. I feel like I did in Dr. Grenner's office. I know Annie's not here, but I can't stop myself from looking around for her.

"Laney," Dad says, putting a hand on each shoulder and shaking me a little. "Laney," he repeats. "We'll find her. I'll help you find her," he assures me. "I know where you used to live. I've sent a letter there with our contact information. If she still lives there she will call us."

"What if she doesn't live there anymore?" I ask.

"We'll deal with that when we come to it," he says.

"How do you know where I used to live?" I ask.

"You pointed to it as we were walking down the street. I panicked, worried that your parents would come out and see you with me. So, I asked if you wanted to play a game. I picked you up and told you to bury your face in my neck and count as high as you could count to see how far I could run while you counted. I ran all the way home, but I drove back later that night to memorize the address, just in case. When we walked in the door, I pretended to Nancy that you were Rebecca and she was so out of touch with reality that she was thrilled. You looked so similar to Rebecca anyway, so it made it easier. She just stepped right back into her role as a mother and started taking care of you. She was happy, I was happy, you were happy. Everything was good again. I packed up the car that night and we drove for hours, I found us a new place to live, I found a new job and we settled in. We started living life again. We tried calling you Rebecca but you cried hysterically every time. You kept saying 'I'm Elly Belly, Annie calls me Elly Belly.' I thought it might be more traumatic for you to try to change your name, so I slowly convinced Nancy to start calling you Elaina, or Laney as a nickname, and you agreed to save Elly as your special name, just for your sister. Nancy was good for a few years, but as time passed, she started to question things. She started to slip back into old memories. She started to realize that you weren't Rebecca. Her pills helped for a while, but she stopped wanting to take them. She wanted to remember Rebecca. She wanted to punish herself for letting her die."

"What about Aunt Sophia and Uncle Victor?" I ask. "Didn't they wonder where Rebecca went and where I came from?"

"We told them about the accident. Of course they were heartbroken for us. They knew how hard we struggled to have a child. They knew how much we loved Rebecca. They lived so far away, we hardly saw them, especially when their kids were young. It was too hard for them to pack up their kids and make the long drive to our house. We had only gone out to see them twice with Rebecca. I think they were afraid to visit us, also, after we lost her. They didn't want to bear witness to our pain first-hand, they didn't want to imagine an accident like that happening to their own children. It was easier for them to stay away. It was easier for all of us. As much as I love my brother, I don't think Nancy or I could have handled seeing them with their two perfect living children and not become overwhelmed with jealousy and anger. We were doing all we could to survive day by day."

He pauses for a moment to scratch Max's head. "I didn't tell them about you right away. At first, I said that we had decided to start the application process for adoption. It wasn't until a year or so later that I finally told them we had been successful in adopting a little girl. They were thrilled for us."

"Did you put the flowers in the forest?"

He nods. "Those were your mother's favourite flowers. When I bought some for her, I bought some for Rebecca, also. I couldn't take them to her resting place, so I thought I could leave them for her close to her mother, in the forest, where no one would see them."

I'm not really listening to his words anymore. *Did Annie send me away because I was a pest?* I wonder, remembering the times she had to get me something to eat, or tie my shoes, or piggyback me home from the park when I was tired. *No. She loved me. I know she did.* "He'll keep you safe," Annie had told me.

"You kept me safe," I say.

"Of course, I did. You're my daughter," he says. "I will always keep you safe."

"Safe from the monster."

"Yes, even safe from the monster," he says. He chuckles and ruffles my hair like I'm a little kid. "Still thinking about the monster in your nightmares, are you?" he asks.

"No, the monster is real," I say. "Annie said you would keep me safe. But she's not safe. The monster will get her."

"What monster?" Dad asks.

I don't know. I only saw the monster's face one, I think. *No, that's not true, is it?*

I saw the monster every day.

CHAPTER 17

Danica

I run to the mailbox as I've done each weekday for the past few months, ever since I received the letter from Elly's dad. I pull the key from my purse. I have a feeling that another letter is coming for me. I couldn't take the chance that Benson would find the next letter, so I had kept the key in my purse the day I received the first letter instead of putting it back in the drawer. That way I could be sure that he could never check the mail. Surprisingly, he didn't even notice. I guess he considers collecting the mail beneath him.

My heart quickens as I stab the key into the hole and turn. *If they send another letter, that is. They wouldn't just give up after one try, would they?*

My hope disappears when I open the door and the mailbox is empty, not even a stupid flyer. Frustrated, I slam the door and turn from it. I kick a stone and it bounces across the sidewalk and pings off the side door of a car parked there. *They have given up,* I think.

I want to scream, pull out my hair, lie down on the ground and pitch a fit like I'm a cranky toddler. Instead, I run. After just a couple of minutes my legs are tired and it feels like I'm breathing fire into my lungs. But I don't stop. I can't stop. I want to run away from everything and everyone.

Why didn't you call when you got the letter, stupid? I berate myself. When I didn't call they probably thought I didn't live here anymore and gave up on me.

I can't see properly; my eyes are blurred from the tears pooled within them. When I stumble and trip, I flap my arms around to catch my balance and stop. I look up and realize I'm standing at the edge of the park. *The* park where I last saw Elly. Where I willingly gave her away to a complete stranger. *What was I thinking?*

I walk over to the playground and climb the steps. It's the first time I've been back to this park since that day. At the top of the slide I kick my shoes and socks off and sit down. I feel Elly's legs wrap around my stomach and her arms weave around my neck, choking me as she clings to me, like I'm her lifeline as we drown together. *We were drowning,* I remind myself, *drowning in Benson's ocean of hate and even our own mother wouldn't help us.*

I think about Elly's face in the photograph. She looks good. I try to smile, try to tell myself I made the right choice for her, but still I feel the guilt eat away at me, feel its teeth chomp down and rip out pieces of my heart, as it has every single moment since I last saw her.

She must have been so scared, I think. *She must have thought I abandoned her, just like our father had abandoned all of us and left our mother vulnerable to the attack of a shark. What had I done that made him leave? Was that why Mom let Benson hurt me, because she was mad at me, too, for chasing Daddy away? Why didn't she protect us?* I wonder. *Why did our mother . . . Why did Crystal bring that monster into her home with two little girls and not even notice what he did to us? Didn't she notice him leave their bed every night? Didn't she see the fear in her daughter's eyes when he was around? Why did she marry him and insist we call him "Daddy"? Was she so broken after our father left that she had completely given up? It wasn't long after Benson's first night in our house that he came into my room.*

How long would it have been before he started climbing into Elly's bed at night, too?

"Neeeeevvvvveeeerrrrr!" I scream out loud, startling myself. I look around and am thankful when I see that I'm alone in the park. A flock of birds erupt from a tree, shaking its branches and knocking some of the leaves to the ground. "You'll never touch Elly," I whisper. "I saved her from you. I saved her from the monster." I feel the pain of my guilt ease slightly, for the first time since that morning. *I saved her from the monster,* I think, picturing her face in the photograph, *and she's had a good life.*

I whip down the slide and for the first time in a long time, I feel free. Benson doesn't know where Elly is. I just need to confirm that and then I could really be free. I could leave knowing that Benson couldn't bring Elly home to replace me.

At the bottom of the slide I dig my toes in the sand. It's cold and hard so I break it up with my toes, feeling the cool sand squish between them. I look up and see his face. George's face. I hadn't known his name, but I had known his heart. I could feel it. I saw it in the way he played with his daughter, the way he seemed to watch over us, too. I knew he wouldn't hurt us.

But he couldn't save both of us. "I can only take one of you," he had said to me. I had known what to do right away. I tried to be strong for her. I didn't want her to be afraid.

I had sat in the park for hours after that, staring down the road, at the very spot where they had disappeared from my sight, where my favourite person in the whole world had vanished from my life forever.

When I finally went back home, I had walked in the door to the usual scene. Mom lying on the couch, Benson sitting beside her with a beer in his hand, watching television. No one seemed concerned that we had been gone for half a day.

"Where's your sister?" Mom had asked, slurring her words, when she was finally able to lift her head enough to look at me.

"Someone took her," I answered.

"No," Mom said, "get her back." She started to sit up.

"Good," Benson said. He popped the lid off a bottle and dropped a pill into his hand. He pushed it into Mom's mouth and titled his beer into her mouth. Then he pushed her back onto the couch. He had raised the bottle to his own lips and chugged back the rest of the beer. "One less mouth for me to feed," he said. "The three of you cost too much for me," he said to Mom. "This is better for me. You go back to sleep."

She had closed her eyes and pulled the blanket back up to her shoulders and she had never spoken Elly's name again. I had never gone back to that park. It was like she had never even existed.

I had raced upstairs and packed up all her clothes, put them into a garbage bag and dragged it out to the curb when Benson was in the bathroom and Mom was passed out.

That night, Benson had told me that he had arranged for Elly to be taken and that if I ever told anyone our secret that all he had to do was make one phone call and she would be back home to replace me. I didn't think that nice man would be friends with someone like Benson, but I had no choice but to believe him. I would have done anything to keep Elly safe. *I did do everything to keep her safe,* I think. A shudder runs through me, causing all my hairs to stand on end.

Was he full of it? Had he scared me with empty threats all these years? It was time to find out.

When I get close enough our house to see that the driveway is empty, I start to run. I don't know how long I'll have before Benson gets home so I have to move quickly.

Mom's asleep on the couch again. I pause and look down at her for a moment. I'm surprised that she actually looks kind of peaceful while she sleeps. I hadn't taken a good look at her in years. *Why would I? She may still live in this house, but she abandoned us just as much as our father did. I won't miss that sight once I'm gone,* I decide.

"Is that you, Danny?" Mom says, lifting her head from the couch cushion when I take a step away from her.

"Yeah, it's me," I say. "Just go back to sleep."

"Come here, would you?" she says. She's struggling to get herself up into a sitting position. She's gasping for breath like she's lifting heavy weights or running a marathon.

"I have something to do," I protest, looking up the stairs. I don't have time for her right now. I want to dig around her bedroom and the basement before Benson gets back. I don't know what I'm looking for, but I'm sure I'll know it when I find it.

"Just for a minute," she says. "I miss you." A bit of drool spills from the corner of her mouth.

Seriously? The first time she makes an effort in years and she picks now to do it.

"Fine," I say and sit down beside her.

We sit there, side by side for a moment. I keep looking straight ahead, but I feel her eyes on me. I refuse to turn to look at her.

She leans her head on my shoulder and lets out a deep sigh. There's almost no weight to her, she's wasted away to skin and bones. "You're so strong," she says. Her words are slow and quiet. She sounds sad. She twists her head and kisses my arm. As much as I hate her, I can't help but be touched by her gesture. Her emotional absence from my life while being physically present has hurt me more than my father abandoning us ever did.

"I miss her so much," she whispers.

I suck in a quick breath and hold it. *She hasn't mentioned Elly once since the day I told her someone took her from the park. Not once.*

"I really messed up after your dad died," she says.

What?

"Dad died?" I ask. My mind starts racing. *He left because I was bad.* I pull away from her and jump off the couch, causing her to twitch and sit up straighter. She looks at me; for the first time in years she looks at me, instead of through me.

"You were so little," she says.

"You said he left us. You lied to me," I accuse. I squeeze my fists together, but force myself to keep them down by my side. I want to punch her in the face and I'm afraid if I move them from my side, I will do just that. I feel pressure build up in my head; my blood is racing through my veins.

"I didn't know how to tell you so that you would understand. I couldn't even understand it. He went to the store to buy milk and never came home. He was killed in a car accident. He did leave us," she says defensively.

I take another step back. "Leaving willingly and being killed in a car accident are two completely different things," I scream at her. "I thought he left because he was mad at me, because I had done something wrong!" I grab on to the coffee table for balance. The floor feels like it's moving in waves underneath my feet. My eyes are blurry, filled with tears, but I can't slow down long enough to try to stop them. I'm about to explode.

"No," Mom says. She starts to laugh, like it's a big joke, but when our eyes meet, her smile instantly disappears. "He loved you so much. The day you were born was the happiest day of his whole life."

"He didn't leave because he was mad at me?" I ask, my voice barely above a whisper.

"No," she says. "Why would you think that?"

"That's what Benson told me," I say.

"Your father lived for you," she says. "You were his whole life. You and your sister," she adds and then erupts into her own fit of hysteria. She's pulling her hair with both hands and drops her face into her lap. She starts kicking her feet and knocks over the coffee table. "What have I done?" she cries. "What have I done?" Then she screams, a gut-wrenching, tortured scream of an animal being devoured by a predator.

I can't watch it anymore. I want to throw myself at her and punch her, scratch her, hurt her. Instead, I force myself to walk backwards until I'm in the front hallway. I pull on my shoes, grab my purse and leave.

Benson lied to me about my father. He has to be lying about Elly, too. I'm going to prove it.

"It's about time," Benson says when I walk through the door. "Where have you been?"

"I had some things to take care of," I say. I hold the plastic bag in my hands behind my back, so he doesn't take it from me. "Hi, Mom," I say sweetly, looking around Benson to her. She looks at me from the couch. Her eyes are empty again, the lifeless glass eyes of a doll. She tries to smile but she looks spaced out.

"Be ready in an hour," he says quietly. "Take a shower, you look like shit."

"Nope," I say. "I'm not doing your stupid show tonight." I walk past him and head upstairs.

"Fine," he says when I reach the top. "I'll pick up Elly and she can do the show tonight." He's followed me from the kitchen, but he stops at the bottom of the staircase. He's leaning on the railing and stretched up toward me. He hisses out the words quietly so that my mother won't hear him.

"Go ahead," I say and smirk down at him, "I dare you to."

"Benny," Mom calls from the couch.

He turns to look at her, anger stretched across his lips.

"I need some more medicine." She reaches for her open pill bottle and knocks it off the coffee table. Little white pills scatter across the floor.

"Stupid," he says and goes to her.

I disappear into my bedroom and pour the contents of the bag on my floor. I bought three door locks. The woman at the hardware store recommended them when I said I needed to be able to lock my door from the inside and make sure that no one could break through. She gave me a funny look at first, but then pointed me straight away to those locks. "They'll work on a regular door," she said. "Put one about a foot from the top, the second one a foot from the bottom and the last one halfway between the two. Hook each lock into its slot and your door won't budge," she said and took three locks from the shelf. She squeezed my hands when she placed the locks in my hands and the look in her eyes told me she was talking from experience.

Quickly, I rip the locks out of their packages and start attaching them to my door and frame with the screwdriver she picked out for me.

Twenty-five minutes later, my hand sore and blistered, I sit back and wait.

CHAPTER 18

Elaina

"Is it her?" I ask, rushing down the stairs.

Dad shakes his head. "No, we don't need new windows, thank you," he says into the phone. "Yes, I'm sure. No, we don't want someone to come out and take a look. I have to go." He's leaning down toward the receiver as he says the final words and hangs up quickly. "It wasn't her," he says, turning to me after the phone is down.

"We're too late," I say. "She doesn't live there anymore, and we'll never find her." *It's my fault,* I think. *How could I have forgotten her. Why did it take me so long to remember her?*

"We'll find her," Dad says.

"She probably won't even want to see me again," I say. "Why would she when I completely forgot about her?"

"If it's anyone's fault, it's mine. You were just a little girl. We will find her," he says. "Now, today is not a day for sadness. You look beautiful, honey." He walks over to me, takes my hand and spins me around.

I smile as I feel my dress twirl around me when I spin. It's a very pretty dress, a beautiful turquoise colour with spaghetti straps and long, flowing, soft material. It reminds me of one of my dresses from dance class when I was little. I used to live in my dance costumes; they made me feel beautiful.

He lifts his camera to his face and starts snapping pictures. "Keep twirling," he says, "it'll look great in the pictures."

I laugh as I twirl, and Max jumps up to dance with me. Then I pick him up and pose for a few more pictures. Dad sets up his tripod and Max and I have to pose again with him.

"Hold on," I say and run to grab a framed picture of Mom to hold in the picture with us for a couple of shots.

"Enough pictures yet?" I complain, but I secretly don't care. I feel like a princess today and I want some pictures to look at later.

He holds out his hand to me and I take it. He leads me outside and to the car.

"Your graduation," Dad says, smiling at me as he opens the door and helps me inside. "I'm so proud of you, honey." He closes the door behind me and walks around.

When we pull into the parking lot, it's practically full, and we have to take a spot at the far end. It takes us a few minutes to walk across the parking lot. The heat from the sun and my nerves about the ceremony have me feeling a little light-headed. I wave my hand across my face to generate a bit of a breeze.

"There you are," Norman says when we walk up to the front door of the school. He's wearing a black suit with a turquoise bow tie that matches my dress, although all I can see under his gown is the bow tie and a little bit of the suit. His graduation cap is on crooked and it makes him look even more adorable. He pulls a huge bouquet of lilies and daisies out from behind his back. "For you," he says and kisses me on the cheek, "so you can feel like you have a little piece of your mom here with you today." I feel heat rise to my face; I don't think I could love him any more. I feel Dad's eyes burning into my back and Norman's lips rest against my cheek for a couple of seconds before he pulls away.

I hear Dad's camera clicking and we turn to pose for a few quick pictures.

"The tent is set up out back—you need to get a cap and gown. People are starting to line up. You have to hurry," he says.

"Have you seen Jenny and Patty?" I ask.

"Yes, they already have their hats and gowns and said they'll meet you in the line-up."

"Dad," I say, turning to him, "can you please hold these for me?"

He reaches out and takes the flowers from me. "Congratulations," he says. He kisses me on the cheek then shakes Norman's hand. "Congratulations to both of you," he says. "I'll go find a seat."

Norman leads me to the cafeteria, which has been converted to a dressing room. I rush over to a table, give them my name and take a gown, quickly wrapping it around my shoulders so that all that remains of my beautiful dress are a few strips of material that dangle below the bottom trim. Norman puts the cap on my head and I laugh as the tassel hits my nose.

"Come with me for a second," Norman says. He takes me by the hand and leads me toward the door that exits to the football field. The set-up for the graduation ceremony is on the opposite side of the school; it will be an outdoor ceremony in the eastern parking lot, where it is held every year.

Our school has some of the best gardens in town. There's a group of old ladies that volunteer their time to garden all spring and summer and one of their kids owns a landscaping company so they get a deal on flowers. They graduated from my school decades ago and have nothing to do now that their kids have grown up and moved away. So, they fundraise all winter to buy plants in the spring to make sure that the graduation ceremony each year will have a beautiful backdrop.

"We don't have time," I protest. "I thought we had to go line up now."

"We have a few minutes," he says. "Look, there are still some people just coming in now. I only need a couple minutes."

I give in and let him lead me out the door.

Outside the air is fresh and wonderful. The sun is shining, the birds are chirping. There is only one thing that would make this day perfect. *Annie.*

We run across the parking lot, toward the football field.

"Remember this spot?" Norman says, as we reach the tree by the bleachers. It's a giant maple tree, the biggest tree on the school grounds. We had actually climbed this tree one day, just a few months after we started dating. Norman had held out his hands to give me a boost and I somehow managed to pull myself up. He then wrapped his arms and legs around the tree like he was some kind of monkey and shimmied his way up. We laughed as we climbed as high as we could through the branches, until the branches were so thin they swayed under our weight.

We sat in that tree for hours, talking about school, our families, our future together, soccer, everything under the sun. I never wanted to leave that tree. Right from the very beginning, I knew he was someone special, someone I could love for the rest of my life.

I laughed as Norman talked to the birds and the squirrels that visited us in the tree that day, squawking at us like we had invaded their home.

Finally, when the sun started to go down, we slowly made our way back down through the branches. But when we got to the lowest branch, it suddenly looked like a long way down. "I'll jump and then I can help you down," Norman said, after we both sat in silence staring at the ground for at least ten minutes.

"No way," I had said, "it's too far. You'll break a leg."

"There's no other choice," he said. "Otherwise we'll be stranded here forever, and I didn't bring any sandwiches."

I had laughed and swatted at his arm. Those days were so carefree. I sometimes wished I could go back to them, before Mom was sick, before my horrible memories of the monster returned to me. *But that was when I didn't remember Annie,* I chastised myself. *I never want to go back to that.*

"Maybe someone will come by and we can ask for help," I had suggested. "Let's just wait a bit and see."

Norman told jokes to distract me from worrying, and it had only taken a couple jokes before all my worries went away. He had a way of always making me feel safe.

Finally, a couple of the old ladies in the gardening club had come by for their evening exercise to walk the track. They heard our screams and one of them raced away while the others came over to talk to us. A few minutes later, the one who had raced away was back to tell us she had phoned the police. A few minutes after that, the first fire truck had arrived to get us down from the tree.

I was horrified. A crowd quickly gathered as the firemen held out their arms for us to jump into. The school photographer took a picture and put it into the school newsletter. After that, the principal had posted warnings all throughout the school that no one was allowed to climb any trees on school property. It was humiliating!

But now that I think back, I laugh at the memory. I've made so many memories with Norman and I wouldn't trade a single one of them.

Now, we're alone except for a squirrel squawking at us from a branch above and a couple standing by the edge of the school, about a hundred feet away. The guy has his back resting on the school wall and the girl is leaning up against him with her back to us. It looks like they're going to make out. *Get a room,* I think.

"Of course," I say. I had been standing there with Jenny and Patty when he had first asked me out. I smile at the memory. "I thought you were going to throw up on me," I said. "You tapped me on the shoulder and when I turned around, your face was some weird shade of green." I giggle.

"Hey, I was nervous." He laughs. "Give a guy a break. Can you blame me?" he asks. "You are so beautiful and wonderful, I never thought you'd agree to go out with a guy like me. But I couldn't live one more day without trying, so I worked up just enough courage to tap you on the shoulder. I had no idea what I was going to say once you turned around."

"And the rest," I say, "is history." I giggle again and look up at the branches of the tree. They jet out in all directions, shooting high up into the sky. I'd spent nearly every lunchtime during high school out by this tree, sometimes sitting on the bleachers near it doing homework, sometimes standing under it chatting with Patty and Jenny or holding hands with Norman. When I looked back at my high school years I would think of this tree as one of my best friends.

I feel a tap on my shoulder and when I turn back around to Norman, he's on one knee. "What are you doing?" I ask, startled.

"Elaina Dawn Samson," he says. "Will you marry me?" He opens a ring box and I see a perfect diamond sparkle and glitter inside.

"What? Are you crazy?" I stammer. "We just finished high school. We're still teenagers." I laugh. It's a nervous laugh.

"I love you, Laney," he says. "I want to marry you. I don't care how old we are. Please say yes." He stands now and reaches out to me. He takes my chin in his hand and raises it so that my mouth meets his. He kisses me. Softly at first, then his intensity builds.

"We have to go," I say, pulling away. "The ceremony will be starting."

"Will you marry me?" he asks again. He's holding on to both of my hands and staring into my eyes.

I haven't even told him about Annie yet, or everything my dad told me. What would he think?

In his gaze, I feel all his love. I feel it mix and intermingle in my heart with all the love I feel for him, and I know in that instant that I want nothing more than to marry him. One day. I know anything I tell him won't ever change any of that. "Yes," I say.

He takes the ring from the box and places it on my finger and gives me another quick kiss on the lips.

"I just have one more question to ask," he says and his face suddenly looks very serious.

"What?" I ask, worried.

"Want to climb this tree with me?" He laughs.

I swat at him as I shout, "No!"

"Okay then." He laughs. "Now, we can go." We run back into the school, through the cafeteria, and take our places in line just as the music starts. He's five people ahead of me and Jenny and Patty are beside each other near the front of the line.

I feel giddy with excitement as I look at my ring. I wave at Jenny and Patty and point to my ring. They squeal, hug each other and clap. Then I realize we have to tell Dad and I feel nauseous. *He's definitely going to think we're too young.* I step along, following the line-up as it moves slowly as each student's name is called. I clap hysterically when Patty then Jenny take their turn to walk across the stage and add in a whistle to my claps when Norman saunters across the stage. I feel like the luckiest girl in the world that he picked me, that he loves me.

When I am second from the front, I look out into the crowd. I find Daddy right away and wave to him. He waves back. Then I continue looking through the crowd. I see Norman's parents and his little brother. I see Patty and Jenny's families. I continue looking. I know she's not in the crowd, but I feel the disappointment build anyway as I scan through the sea of faces and don't see the one face I really want to see.

Oh, Annie. I sigh. *Please call. I need to see you again one day.*

"Elaina Dawn Samson," the principal calls and I walk out up the stairs and across the stage that has been set up under the tent.

Don't trip, don't trip, I repeat and watch each step I take.

The principal hands me my diploma and shakes my hand. I continue down the row, shaking hands with the teachers arranged there. Some I know very well, and some I barely recognize. My favourite teacher, Mrs. Zackary, reaches forward and gives me a big hug. After the last handshake I turn and hold up my diploma. I smile for the photographer. The crowd cheers. I see Dad stand up, clapping furiously.

A movement behind him catches my eye. I look past him, to the edge of the school grounds. There is a line of shrubs, about four feet tall, that stretches along the perimeter of the school grounds. A woman and a man are standing there. Watching our ceremony. I didn't see them there before. They just appeared when I walked across the stage. I look at the woman, wishing I had super vision. All I can make out is her long, dark hair, similar to mine. *Annie?*

"Annie!" I shout out, waving at her. My cry startles the photographer, causing him to jump slightly, knocking his camera off the tripod. He scrambles to catch it before it hits the ground. "Annie!" I shout again.

The woman ducks behind the shrubs and disappears from sight. An instant later I see the man being pulled downward, until he, too, is gone from sight. *It is her!*

"Annie!" I yell again and run toward her, forgetting that I am five feet up on a makeshift stage. An instant later, the floor disappears out from under me and everything turns black.

CHAPTER 19

Danica

I pull the invitation from my pocket. It's plain, just a few words scribbled on a piece of paper with a date, time and address of the school. *Elly's graduation.* I rub my fingers over her name on the piece of paper. It came in the mail seven days ago, almost a year after the original letter. *They hadn't given up on me.* I keep that letter and the picture of Elly taped to the bottom of my dresser so that Benson will never find them. I'm sure he goes through my room when I'm out, but I didn't believe he is smart enough to actually look under the drawers.

The test I had done with the locks had worked. I had sat on my bed, laughing, when he came to my room that night. The doorknob twisted back and forth furiously and I heard a thud each time he threw his body up against my door. But the woman had been right: my door didn't budge. I heard Benson swear from outside my room, then stomp away. A few minutes later I heard his car door slam and he peeled out of the driveway, squealing his tires.

I had run to the bathroom and to the kitchen to grab a box of granola bars and crackers and I filled two cups with water, then locked myself back in my room. I sat by the window, barely breathing, until I heard him pull up into the driveway hours later.

My heart did a little dance when he was the only one to step out of his car. Just to be safe, I had stayed in my room for four more days, only leaving it to go to the bathroom when Benson's car wasn't in the driveway. He never brought Elly home.

On the last day, I had woken up and his car was gone, so I quickly undid my locks and ran to the bathroom. When I flushed the toilet and opened the door he was standing there. It had been a trap; the bastard had outsmarted me and parked his car down the road.

He had beaten me up, badly, and taken the locks off my door. After a week to recover, mostly to let the bruises fade, he had put me back to work. It had seemed a little more bearable, though, to be under his control when his threats only included my own pain and suffering. He no longer threatened to bring Elly home to replace me. I knew then that it was only a matter of time until I was out of there. I just needed a plan.

Then the invitation had arrived.

I can't go to her graduation, can I? I think, caressing the invitation between my fingers as I walk across the library, headed for a seat at a computer.

I type the address into the computer. I couldn't risk looking it up at home, in case Benson checked the computer history, which I'm sure he did. A map pops up and says that her school is a seven hour and thirteen minute drive away. Of course, that's taking into consideration posted speed limits, so I could probably knock at least an hour off of that—well, if I actually knew how to drive, that is.

I look at the clock. The ceremony starts in nine hours and twenty-seven minutes. I leave the library and start walking.

How could I get there? Steal Benson's car? He'd kill me when I got back. What if I never came back? Yeah, right, like I'll just show up at her graduation and Elly will take me home to live with her like I'm a pathetic, lost puppy. No way. Besides, I'm a mess, I could never let her see me like this. And I've never been allowed to get a driver's licence, so if I got pulled over, I'd not only miss her ceremony, but be in even bigger trouble.

I had taken off this morning wearing just an old pair of jeans and a raggedy T-shirt. I didn't even put on makeup or dry my hair. A wicked smile crosses my lips when I think about Benson passed out on the couch as I walked out the door that morning. I had crumbled up a couple of pills, the same ones he force-fed my lame excuse for a mother, dissolved them in a bottle of beer and handed it to him the moment he woke up. The only good thing about living with a drunk was that he didn't even question me when I handed him a beer before he had even taken his morning pee.

I had waited, watching as he took the first gulp, just to make sure he didn't notice a change in the taste from the pills. When he chugged down half the bottle, burped, scratched his butt, then ordered me to grab him another beer, I knew I was safe. I jumped in the shower and by the time I had pulled on some old clothes from the hamper, he was out cold.

I wasn't about to wait around to see how long the pills would last, so I grabbed my purse, a few twenties from Benson's wallet and Crystal's phone and took off.

Why had I never thought of this before? It was brilliant.

I'm still walking, not sure where I'm headed. *I need a plan.*

I need to see Elly, I need to know that she's okay. So, if I can't let her see me, maybe I can just see her. Watch from a distance. She'll never even know I'm there. Yes, that's what I'll do.

The thought of seeing Elly, for the first time in almost fifteen years, sends a thrill through me and I start skipping down the street. Suddenly everything is brighter. The sun peeks out from behind a cloud, enveloping me with warmth and brightness, like a protective shield has just been placed around my shoulders for the first time in my life. The birds chirp louder. Squirrels scurry about, running past the sidewalk in front of me. I notice flowers in bloom all around me.

I know it must be a sign that I've made the right choice. *I'm going to Elly's graduation,* I think excitedly. I continue to skip down the sidewalk until I get to the corner, where the light is red. *Now for my plan,* I think.

As I wait, I look across the road and realize I do have a plan. I've had a plan since the moment I left the library, although I didn't realize it until this moment, when I look across the street and see Hammers & Nails Hardware.

Brent.

He's the only person I would ever trust to help me.

I haven't seen him since that awful night. I shudder at the memory and my stomach knots when I picture his busted-up face, courtesy of Benson. I had asked around about him after that, to make sure he was okay, but I didn't seek him out, and he didn't look for me the rest of the summer.

I cried the day I heard he had gone back to school, but I knew it was best. For him, at least.

Did he even come home this summer? And if so, did he come back to work at the same hardware store? It's worth a shot. It's my only shot.

I cross the parking lot. I pause outside the front doors for a moment to catch my breath. I curse myself now for not taking a couple of minutes to put on some makeup, or at least do something with my hair. *There's no time. It's now or never,* I think and step into the doorway. I set off the sensors that open the big glass doors and take a step inside.

I walk up and down every aisle, twice, without luck. *Shoot. He's not here.* Angry at myself for getting my hopes up, I whip around, ready to run down the aisle and out the door before I lose it. *I won't see Elly after all.*

I crash into someone who had been carrying a stack of boxes. Boxes fly into the air, crash down on the floor and bust open, spilling nails all over the floor.

"Sorry," I say and bend down to pick up a handful of nails. When I stand to hand over the nails, I drop them again. Brent is standing right in front of me, and looks as shocked to see me as I feel to see him.

I start sobbing and throw myself at him, wrapping my arms around him and burying my face into his neck. Even wearing a beige apron with a little "Brent" nametag, he looks amazing. "I'm sorry, I'm so sorry," I cry. I can't stop picturing him that last night I saw him.

"Danica," he says. My heart lifts when he hugs me back. A part of me had been afraid he would turn away from me if our paths ever did cross again.

"I'm sorry," I say again.

"It's okay, Danica," he says, pulling away from me. He puts his hands on my shoulders and looks into my eyes. "I'm okay, Danica. Look at me, I'm fine."

He does look fine. He looks great, actually. I take a deep breath and force myself to get it together.

"What are you doing here?" he asks. His hands are still on my shoulders.

"Looking for you," I say.

"Why?"

"I need your help."

He pauses for a moment then says, "Whatever you need, you got it."

"Turn right up there," I say, pointing to the road ahead. I look down at the map on his phone. "It's on this road. When you see the school, just park anywhere. Don't get too close to it. The ceremony starts in half an hour, we have to hurry." I'm feeling high with excitement. *I'm going to see Elly.*

"I don't know why you want to watch from the sidelines," he says.

"I told you," I say, "I don't want her to see me like this. She'd be disappointed."

He slows the car and swerves it against the curb. "We're good here."

We both get out and start walking.

"You're anything but a disappointment," he says and takes my hand. He continues to hold it as we walk. "You're beautiful and smart and funny," he says, "and she'd be thrilled to see you."

I punch him in the arm with my free hand, pretending to be embarrassed by his compliments, but my heart is soaring. *He thinks I'm beautiful.*

"There," I say, pointing up ahead, "let's cut across the football field."

We cross the street.

"What if you need a ticket to get inside?" he asks.

"Oh, I never thought of that," I say. *Was all this for nothing?* I feel tears spring to my eyes, and I stop walking.

"Don't worry," he says, "maybe it'll be outside. It's a nice day. Yes"—he's making an attempt to sound confident—"I'm sure it'll be outside. You will see Elly get her diploma, even if we have to climb the roof and watch from a skylight." He tugs on my hand and we start walking again. He checks his watch. "We only have a few minutes," he says and pulls me off the football field and onto the pavement.

I'm standing two feet away from Elly's school. I reach out and touch the wall with the palm of my hand. My heart is beating so hard I can feel it in my throat.

Suddenly a door opens and two people, a boy and a girl, burst through it.

Brent pulls me against him and backs up against the school. He leans in toward me and I think he's going to kiss me. Instead, he moves my head to the side and peers around me. I silently laugh at myself for thinking he still wanted to kiss me. *At least he's here helping me; that's more than I should even ask for.*

"It's two graduates," he whispers into my ear. "They're wearing their caps and gowns. Did we look that dorky on graduation day?"

He chuckles then stops when he remembers I didn't go to our graduation ceremony. His lips are buried in my hair and just graze my ear. I feel my knees get wobbly, so I lean into him for support. *That's all I need is to pass out now,* I think.

"They've stopped by a tree," he says. They can't be very far away, I can hear their voices, although I can't make out all the words they're saying.

I start to turn around, but he pulls me against him again.

"Just give them a minute," he says. "They'll have to go back inside, and we'll run around back."

The instant I hear it, my body goes limp.

"Whoa," Brent says and catches me.

"It's her," I whisper. "It's Elly." The memory of her laughter floods my senses. I can hear her laughter. I can feel her laughter. It's exactly as I remember it. *The sweetest sound I've ever heard.*

"How do you know?"

"Her laugh," I say. I'm trembling and tears are spilling down my cheeks. I can't breathe. "I'd recognize it anywhere." The only thing that is keeping me from running to her is the shame and embarrassment of who I am. Of who Benson has made me.

"Take a breath and calm down," Brent says. "I'm going to turn us around, so you can take a look. Keep holding on to me. Pretend you're whispering into my ear, so they don't see you staring at them."

He practically lifts me off the ground to turn us around. As soon as I see her, smiling and happy, I know I made the right choice in the park all those years ago. *She looks happy. Full of life. Safe.*

The boy she's with bends down on one knee. He's holding out a ring box to her. I feel like I'm flying, thrilled to be witness to this moment. Moments later he's placing the ring on her finger and kissing her sweetly.

I bury my face into Brent's neck as they run past us, hand in hand, and disappear into the school.

When Brent pulls away from me, I see that his face is damp, too. I think it's my tears that have rubbed off onto his cheeks, but his eyes are wet. *He's crying with me.* In that moment I'm reminded again that I will love him until the day I die.

"Let's go," he says, wiping his eyes with the back of his arm. "It's almost time."

We sniffle as we run, across the school and around the back corner. We stop quickly when we see the giant tent, and rows upon rows of people in the audience. There is a makeshift stage up front, and a podium. Teachers are lined up across the stage, and there is a student walking across the stage.

"Look," Brent says, pointing. "If we run to the edge of the property, we can hide behind those shrubs. It's far enough that you can still see her. We'll be behind all the seats—no one will notice us out there."

"Okay," I say, "let's go."

We speed-walk diagonally across the property, away from the ceremony, and when we get to the edge, we cut back along the sidewalk. At the shrubs, we stop. "Duck down," I say.

We both squat behind the bushes.

With the microphone, we can hear the voices being called out.

A bead of sweat drips off my head and lands on the sidewalk. I stare at the darkened spot on the ground as we wait. I'm counting, reminding myself to breathe.

"Elaina Dawn Samson," we hear over the microphone.

Brent and I both stand up.

Elly gracefully climbs the steps and walks across the stage. She looks like she's talking to herself as she takes her diploma and moves along the stage, shaking hands with all the teachers and stopping to hug one as she works her way through the line-up. At the end of the line-up of teachers, she turns and faces the crowd. A photographer snaps her picture. A man in the crowd stands up, clapping furiously. She waves to him. For a second I think she's waving at me. I panic and jump. I bump into Brent and we fall forward, into the bushes.

We straighten ourselves and I look up again, at Elly. Now I'm sure she's waving at me. "Annie!" she screams.

Oh my God.

"Annie!" she screams again and steps forward on the stage. I duck down. Brent is still standing, so I reach up and pull him down with me.

"We have to get out of here," I say. Still bent over at the waist, I start to run. I don't stop until we've passed the edge of the shrubs and are in front of a house.

We stand up straight and continue to run. I'm laughing and coughing from running so fast. I feel like I'm flying. *I've seen her. She looks amazing.*

We keep running, through the neighbourhood and back around the school, eventually making our way back to the car. We climb inside and Brent drives off. We're still laughing and trying to catch our breath.

"Where to now?" he asks. "We can't make it back tonight. It's too long of a drive."

I'm sure Benson is awake by now. *He'll be pissed that I'm not home. But Elly is safe and that's all that matters. He doesn't know where she is. She's an adult now anyway; he can't just pick her up and take her to his home. I'm free.*

I look over at Brent and he winks at me. I feel my heart flutter. This is the best day of my entire life.

We drive for a couple hours in a happy silence. I feel the car slow and the blinkers click. "We'll stay here tonight," Brent says, pulling into the parking lot of a little motel. It's old and run down. The light bulbs behind the *cy* on the Vacancy sign are out. The trash can by the front door is overflowing with garbage.

We will stay here together. It's perfect.

I wait in the car while Brent gets us a room. He's grinning when he climbs back in beside me. He pulls into a parking spot and we get out. The room is small. There's a double bed with floral bedding, a lamp on a side table, and a small TV on a three-drawer dresser.

Brent locks the door and steps toward me.

My knees start to feel wobbly.

He reaches out and brushes the hair from my shoulder, exposing my neck. "I've always loved you, Danica," he says and leans into me. When his lips touch my skin at the base of my neck, an electrical current shoots through me and makes the room spin. When we kiss, I feel myself float up off the ground, into the sky, into my wildest dreams.

Although Benson and his friends have used me and violated me for as long as I can remember, for the first time in my life, I feel love when Brent touches me. He kisses each one of my scars, his warm lips gently healing and releasing the pain locked away behind each one. In my heart, there has never been anyone but him.

He wraps his arms around me and holds me against him.

"I can't take you back to that monster again," he says. He chokes the words out.

"I'm not going back," I say. "Ever."

CHAPTER 20

Elaina

"It was her," I say, "it was Annie. I just know it." I fold my arms across my chest and stare at him.

"Sweetie," Dad says. He's looking at me like I'm a stupid little kid. "We've been over this a hundred times. It wasn't Annie. She hasn't called. She would have called if she were coming to your graduation. She wouldn't just show up and not talk to you."

"I know it was her." I pout.

"You bumped your head when you fell off the stage. There's probably some swelling that's affecting the images in your memory. Come here, let me see if you've still got a bump on your head." He laughs as he waves me over.

"My brain is not bruised. It was her," I insist.

"She hasn't called in response to my letter or the invitation to your graduation. We need to accept the very likely possibility that she doesn't even live at that address anymore. If she still lived there, we would have heard from her."

"Unless she can't answer," I say. "What if someone is hiding her mail? Or holding her hostage?" I throw my hands up to cover my face. *Was it really her?*

"Enough of this nonsense for now," Dad says. "We have to get moving. How many more boxes do you have to bring down?"

"I don't want to go away for school. What if Annie calls?" Max saunters over to me and plops down by my feet. He leans against my leg for support.

"I will be here if she calls," he says. "Ah," he says, holding up his hand in front of my face just as I'm about to raise my voice in protest. "And *if* she does, I will call you the very second I hear from her. I'll call you from my cell while she is on our home line. If she calls, I will tell her to come straight over and I'll tie her to the kitchen table and send a race car taxi driver to pick you up from school. Day or night, cross my heart and hope to die," he says and laughs.

"Now you're just making fun of me." I pout again, pushing my bottom lip out extra far to make him feel bad.

"You can't make yourself crazy over this, Laney. I'm sure Annie is fine, and we will find her one day. You have to have faith in that. In the meantime, life goes on. You're starting university, it's exciting. Come on, let's see a smile," he urges. "You've been talking about this day since your first day of high school."

I stare at him blankly.

"Well then," he says, clapping his hands together, "do you need help bringing anything else down?"

"No, all that's left is my suitcase." I bend down to rub Max's belly. He flops over onto the floor. His leg shakes as I scratch his belly, but he's old now, so his leg is moving much slower than it used to. "I can't leave Max," I say. "Look at him. He's too old for this kind of upheaval in his life. He won't understand. He'll think I abandoned him."

"You'll be home for visits," Dad says. "Max can last until then. Thanksgiving and Christmas are just around the corner. Then there's Reading Week in February. Before you know it you'll be back home for the summer. Max won't even have time to miss you and I'll take good care of him."

"Will you rub his belly every night until he falls asleep?"

"I promise," Dad says.

"Will you tell him he's a good boy when he comes when you call?"

"Of course."

"Will you give him extra treats if he looks like he's missing me?"

"Absolutely." Dad sighs.

"Will you—"

"Enough, Laney," Dad says. "I know how to take care of a child and a dog. Max will be just fine."

I scrunch my face and stick my tongue out at him as he turns his back to me. Then I bend to give Max a final belly rub. "Maybe I'll just pack you in my suitcase and take you with me," I say to him and kiss his nose. His tails thumps against the floor as he wags it. Then I run upstairs to get my suitcase.

Ten minutes later we're sitting in the car. The back seat and trunk are full of suitcases and boxes that I'm going to take with me. "I have a bad feeling about this," I say as Dad pulls out of the driveway. I turn and look back at our house, watching it get smaller and smaller as we drive down the road.

"Me, too," Dad says, and I immediately start to panic. "I don't think you're going to have room for all of this stuff and I'm going to be carting half of it back home."

I look over at him. When I don't smile, his quickly disappears.

"Come on, Laney," he says. "It's a new chapter in your life, it's normal to be nervous about it."

"I'm not nervous about going to school," I say. "I have this feeling that Annie needs me. That she needs my help."

"Until she contacts us, there's no way to know for sure," Dad says. "We have to move on, keep living our own lives. If it's meant to be, she will contact us one day, when she's ready." He smiles at me, but I just cross my arms and let out a big grunt.

"What if she doesn't live there anymore? What if she hasn't received your letters?"

"I'll hire a private investigator."

"You don't even know her last name," I argue.

"Doesn't matter," he says. "Somehow we will find her."

"Why can't I just stay home and go to school nearby? Why are you trying to get rid of me?"

"I'm not trying to get rid of you, Laney. I just want you to get out and experience life. You can't sit around at home waiting for the phone to ring. Get out, meet new people, see new things. You're a good kid, Laney, you deserve to have some fun."

"Hmm," I grumble. I fold my eyes, turn my back to him slightly and stare out the window for the rest of the drive.

"That way," I shout, pointing to a parking lot full of cars and people walking through it. Carts are piled high as kids laugh, excitement flowing through them, and parents' faces show a combination of relief, excitement and worry for their babies that they'll be leaving behind.

"See, I don't have that much stuff compared to everyone else," I say, pointing to two different sets of families that are standing beside an enormous stack of boxes and suitcases.

"There's Norman!" I shout.

"Oh, goodie," Dad says sarcastically.

"Drive around that car and pull up over there," I command.

"I do know how to drive, Laney, did you forget that?"

I ignore him and wave my arm frantically through my open window. "Norman!" I shout.

He waves and smiles when he sees me and trots toward our car.

"Why did he have to choose the same school as you?" Dad grumbles. "You've already agreed to marry him, can't he give you some space to allow you to make sure it's what you really want?"

"It is what I want, Dad, and we decided together which schools to apply to so that we could make sure that we were together."

"Yeah, yeah," he says. He's the one sulking now.

I hop out of the car and run toward Norman, leaping into his arms, and I give him a long, hard kiss. Then I turn around, and smile and wave at Dad.

Norman and Dad unload the car and start a pile while I pick up my keys and a cart.

When I get back to the car, they're both looking over at a big commotion up ahead. A group of guys start cheering and yelling. We watch as they raise a sign, a bed sheet spray-painted with black letters that says, "Take a hike, dads, your daughters are ours now."

Dad sputters and chokes. The guys ahead of us jump and high-five each other, laughing and whistling at a group of girls as they walk by.

Two security guards walk quickly toward the boys and motion to their sign. Their laughter stops and the sign quickly falls to the ground.

"Um, yeah, um, on second thought, maybe you don't have to go here . . ." Dad says. His face goes white as the blood drains from it. He's staring at the bed sheet sign, crumpled on the ground. "You know, there is a nice school within driving distance of home. Maybe I can buy you a car and you can just live at home."

"Oh, but Daddy," I taunt, "I must get out and start living my life. You know, new people, new experiences. A wise man once told me that." I laugh and blow a kiss at him and turn to start loading my cart. *Let him suffer*, I think and laugh to myself.

He's still frowning, but he helps me load up my cart and take up the first load while Norman guards the rest of my stuff.

"So, you promise you'll hire a private investigator?" I ask after Dad's carried up the last box. Norman's gone; he made up some excuse about needing to clean his room after we had the last load on the cart and Dad moved his car over into the parking lot. I knew he just wanted to give me some space to say goodbye to my dad. He's pretty good that way; he just seems to know when I need something.

"Yes, Laney, for the tenth time, I promise." He sighs.

"If she doesn't call by tomorrow, you'll call around to find one?"

"Laney, be reasonable. You have to consider the possibility that Annie doesn't want to contact us."

"Why wouldn't she?" I ask. "I know she would want to see me again." *Wouldn't she?*

"I'll tell you what," Dad says. "If we don't hear from her by the end of your first year of school—"

"By the end of September," I interrupt.

"By the end of your first semester then," he continues. "Then I'll drive to the house personally to see if she lives there. If she does, I will drag her home with me. If she doesn't, I will hire a private investigator to search the ends of the earth until we find her. Agreed?"

"And you won't stop until we find her." I hold out my fist, pinky extended toward him.

He looks at my hand and raises his eyebrow. "Seriously?"

"Yes, seriously," I say, thrusting my hand toward him.

A strange look crosses his face as he looks at my hand. "Why are you looking at me like that?" I ask.

"It's just . . . you remind me of your sister right now. She made me pinky swear to protect you. Now you're doing the same for her." He smiles and wraps his pinky in mine. "Pinky swear," he says. "I will search high and low. I will search far and wide. I will look under every rock, behind every tree. I will not stop until we find her."

I know he's trying to make light of my promise, but I also know he means every word of it. He has never broken a promise to me in his life.

I jump up toward him and wrap my arms around him. I feel a sudden rush of emotions and I start to cry so I bury my face in his neck. "I'm going to miss you, Dad," I sob.

"Oh, Laney," he says, squeezing me. "I'm going to miss you so much, honey. You'll have a great time at school, you'll see. You'll love it."

CHAPTER 21

Danica

"Good morning, Mrs. Dennings," Brent says, kissing my ear. He moves his arm across my bulging belly.

"I'm not Mrs. Dennings yet." I laugh.

"I know, I'm just practicing," he says. "I like the sound of it. How did my baby sleep?" He kisses the back of my neck.

"Kicked me all night and kept me awake," I grumble. But I'm not angry. I'm thrilled to be pregnant with Brent's baby. I turn to him and smile. I know I will be a good mother, despite the horrible example I grew up with. I will love and protect my baby.

"I'm making breakfast," he says. "French toast sprinkled with cinnamon and icing sugar. It'll be ready when you get out of the shower."

Fifteen minutes later I'm sitting at the table with him. I look around our apartment and smile. It's small, with one bedroom, a tiny kitchen and living room. Not even enough room for a table, so we eat our meals on the couch. But we've made it a home. It's the first home I've ever felt safe in.

Brent had a little bit of money saved, so he used it to get us this apartment. We both found jobs right away when we decided to stay in this town after our one night in the hotel. Brent was working at a diner in the kitchen. It was long hours, but the pay was decent, and he sometimes got to bring home leftovers. He also enjoyed practicing at home, which meant he did most of the cooking.

I had found a job in a salon, sweeping up hair, washing hair, and booking appointments for the hairdressers. The people there were nice, and the hours were regular.

We had been saving up so that we could get a bigger apartment someday and buy some nice things for the baby.

"I can pick up an extra shift tonight," Brent says.

"Okay," I say, "I'll take the bus home." I take a bite of the French toast and moan. "This is delicious."

"Are you sure?" he says. "I can get someone else to take the shift."

"I'll be fine," I assure him. "We could use the extra money."

"Okay," he says. "But the money from this shift is going in the wedding fund."

"Don't be silly," I say. "We'll need diapers and clothes and baby food and a car seat and toys." I start to hyperventilate. "Are you sure we can do this?" I ask. "Babies are expensive."

"Of course, we can do this," he says. He's up off the couch and kneeling in front of me, his head resting gently on my belly. I raise my plate and rest it on top of his head. "We can do anything." He rubs my belly. "I love you, baby," he says to my belly and kisses it.

I feel the baby kick.

"Ow!" He laughs. "He kicked me right in the chops. He's a strong little guy."

I move my plate as he pulls away, rubbing his jaw and laughing.

"What makes you think it's a boy?" I ask, rubbing my belly. The baby is still kicking. "I think it likes your cooking." I laugh.

"Maybe it's a girl," he says and shrugs. "With your beautiful eyes and cute little nose. We can name her after your sister. If you want to."

I smile. He's the most thoughtful person I've ever known.

"But," he says, "I want you to be my wife. The sooner the better. So, the extra money from tonight's shift is going into the wedding fund."

"We don't have to get married," I say.

"Of course, we do," he says. "Unless you don't want to?" He looks panicked.

"I want to," I say.

"Good, then it's settled," he says. "Hold out your hand."

I hold out my hand, palm up.

"Other way," he says, turning my hand over. He reaches into his pocket and pulls out a ring.

"I promised you a real diamond one day," he says and slides the ring onto my finger. My fingers are a little swollen, so he has to force it on.

I raise my hand to admire the ring. It's a single diamond held by four claws. "It's beautiful," I whisper. *What did I ever do to deserve him?* I wonder. "You can't afford this," I protest.

"I can and I did. I promised you a real diamond one day," he says and leans over my belly to kiss me, "and I keep my promises to you."

"It's just, we won't have much of a wedding," I say. "Your parents disowned you when you said you weren't going back to school. There's no way I'm inviting my mother or Benson. We won't have any guests." I sigh. If it weren't for Brent I would be completely alone.

"We can invite Elly," he suggests. "And her father."

I think Brent assumes the man we saw at the graduation was Elly's real dad. He had never asked about why Elly didn't live with us and I had never volunteered the information. It was too hard to talk about. I didn't even like thinking about it. I had handed her over to a complete stranger when she was three years old. *What kind of monster did that make me? But it had all worked out.*

I had recognized the man in the park. I'd seen him there so many times with a little girl, about Elly's age. She had long, dark hair and even looked a little like Elly. She always had fun in the park; the man would push her on the swings and catch her at the bottom of the slide. She would laugh and hold his hand and smile when she looked at him. I knew he had to be a good dad.

I also knew our house wasn't safe for Elly. I had been protecting her by teaching her to remain silent up in the top bunk while I didn't fight Benson when he came into our room at night. It hadn't always been like that. Our real daddy was nice to us. Mom was happy then. They would both take us to the park, and they would play games with us.

The last time I saw my dad we had been playing in the living room while Mom was in the shower. Daddy and I squished Elly between us into an "Elly Sandwich" and she giggled so much that tears dripped down her rosy cheeks. Dad and I were laughing, too.

Daddy looked over at me. "You're a great big sister, Danica," he said. "Elly's a lucky girl. You must always look out for her and protect her. That's your job as her big sister." He had stopped smiling and sounded serious, so I paid close attention to him and nodded.

"It's your job to keep her safe. Do you hear me?" he asked.

I nodded again.

"Great," he said and held up his fist with his pinky sticking out. "Pinky swear to seal the deal."

I wrapped my pinky around his. "Pinky swear," I said.

He wiggled our hands together until Elly burst out in a fresh batch of giggles and we both joined her.

I didn't know it then, but in that moment, life was perfect.

Mom got out of the shower and wanted a coffee. We were out of milk so Daddy had said he would run to the store to get it after he put us to bed.

He tucked us in, gave us each a kiss and told us he loved us. Then he closed the door behind him, and I never saw him again.

The next morning, Mom was locked in her bedroom. I could hear her crying, but she wouldn't come out and I couldn't turn her door handle to open the door. She stayed that way for a long time. I stayed home from school and took care of Elly while Mom cried in her room.

Elly and I cried outside her door, asking where Daddy was, but she never answered us.

Then one night she opened her bedroom door, put makeup on in the bathroom while we watched, tucked us into bed and told us not to get out. When we woke up in the morning Benson was there and he had been there ever since.

He was nice to us at first, but it hadn't lasted long. When he hurt me I tried not to cry; I didn't want to scare Elly. I had tried to tell Mom, but one day she sat us both down and said Benson was our daddy now and we just had to do what he said because he would take care of all of us now that our real daddy had left us.

That man in the park had seemed nice. He looked like he took good care of the little girl. I took a chance. At the age of five years old, I was forced to gamble with my little sister's life. From what I saw at her graduation ceremony, my gamble had paid off.

"Hello," Brent says. "Earth to Danica." He's waving his hand in front of my face. "Where'd you go?"

"Oh, sorry," I say, coming back to the present.

"So," he says, "should we invite Elly?"

"No," I say, shaking my head. "That's not a good idea."

"Sure it is," he says. "I'm sure she'll invite you to her wedding."

I feel the blood drain from my face. "You're right," I say. My body starts shaking, shivering like I'm freezing cold.

"Hey, hey," he says, rubbing my arm. "What's wrong? It's a good thing if she invites you."

"Where will she send the invitation?"

He catches up. "Oh," he says. "Maybe it's time to contact her. Give her an updated address at least, if you're not ready to see her yet."

"The graduation invitation only had the school address on it. Her dad's phone number was on the letter. The letter is still at the house. I don't know how to contact her." I'm immediately overcome with panic. "What if she's already sent another letter to the house, to Benson."

"Slow down a second," Brent says, putting a hand on my shoulder. "I'll see if I can find their phone number. You finish your breakfast—by the time you're done I'm sure I'll have his phone number." He jumps up and turns on the computer.

I look down at my French toast. My appetite is gone.

"The baby needs the food," he urges.

I stab my fork into another piece and chew. It's not as delicious anymore. All I can think about is Elly mailing a wedding invitation to me at Benson's house. He would know exactly where to find her.

"Shoot," Brent says. "He must be unlisted. I can't find a phone number for him."

My stomach knots, forcing my breakfast back up. Luckily, I catch it with my plate. "We have to go back there, to the house," I say. "I need to get the letter so I can call them. They need to know not to mail anything else to that house."

"We'll go," Brent says. "We'll go," he repeats. "Calm down. We need to think this through. We'll have to get the police to come with us."

"No," I say. "No police." *They'll ask questions. I can't talk about what Benson did to me. I don't want to think about it ever again. I don't want anyone to ever know about it.*

"Well, then we'll have to be careful. Watch the house first, make sure he's gone before we go in. We're both off tomorrow, we'll leave in the morning."

We've been sitting down the road from the house for almost eight hours. Benson's car is in the driveway. It hasn't moved all day. After two and a half hours, my mother came out and walked down the road. Almost an hour later she returned, carrying a case of beer. *Lazy jerk wouldn't even let her use his car to run his errands,* I thought. I watched her as she struggled with the beer, stopping every couple of minutes to put it down to rest. She looked old and haggard. But at least she was off the couch. Maybe Benson had stopped keeping her in a drugged state now that he needed her to run his errands for him. *Lazy jerk.*

Good thing Brent thought ahead and packed some food. I pull out some crackers and another water and start nibbling. I'm always hungry these days.

"Ah crap," I say. "I need to pee again."

"Can you hold it?" he asks.

"Not for long."

"You should just wait at the coffee shop." Brent laughs. "Then you can pee whenever you need to. Besides, maybe it's not a good idea for you to go in the house."

"I don't want you to go in there," I say, remembering Benson's last threat. *Next time you step into my house, you're dead.* I shudder at the thought. I can't take that chance. "I'll go in and get the letter. You wait in the car."

"I'm quicker," he teases, placing his hand on my bulging belly. "I'll go in and get the letter and zip right back out. Two minutes tops."

"No." I say firmly. "There's no room for negotiation here."

"Fine," he says. "I'll take you to the bathroom."

We pull out and drive down the block. Ten minutes later we're back in our surveillance spot. Luckily, no one had taken it as it gave us a perfect view of the driveway. There were cars parked all over the road, some cars had come and gone but there were a couple of cars that had been there all day, so no one should look twice at our car being there.

"His car is gone," I say.

"Shoot," Brent says.

"I wonder how long he's been gone."

"We should wait," Brent says. "We don't have any idea where he went—he could be coming back any minute."

"We don't have time to wait," I say, pulling on the door handle. "I need to get that letter. It's getting dark, they'll be staying in drinking the rest of the night I'm sure. Elly or her dad could send another letter here any time that would lead Benson right to their doorway. I can't risk it. I'm going in." I step out and close the door.

Brent rolls down the window. "I'm coming with you."

"No," I say. "The stakes are too high. Benson will kill you if he comes home and catches you in there."

"And what do you think he'll do to you?" he asks.

"I'll be okay," I assure him. "He'll be rattled because I've been gone, but he can't hurt me anymore." *Unless he kills you,* I think. "Just promise me you'll stay here."

"Fine," he grumbles. "But if his car pulls up and you're not back outside within two minutes, I'm coming in."

"No," I say.

"That's the only deal," he says.

"Okay, fine," I agree and turn and walk away. I waddle down the road, thinking that Brent was right about one thing: he is a lot faster than I am these days.

I know my mother is inside, with any luck she'll be passed out again. I turn the knob on the front door and am happy it's unlocked. I step inside. My heart is beating so hard I can hear the thumping in my ears. The baby is flip-flopping around, kicking me in the ribs and the bladder. *I have to pee again.*

I peer around the corner and Mom is not on the couch. I take the stairs slowly, stepping as lightly as possible each time, hoping that I don't make them creak too loud. I pass her bedroom. It's empty. I hear the toilet flush. I take a few quick steps forward then pass the bathroom door quickly as the water is running in the sink. *I hope that's Crystal in there,* I think. I suddenly panic, thinking that Benson could have sent my mom out in the car this time. It was stupid of me to come in without knowing for sure that Benson was gone along with his car.

I step into my old bedroom and wait behind the door, peeking through the crack as the bathroom door opens. I can breathe again when I see my mother come out and go into her bedroom, pulling the door shut behind her.

I step lightly across my bedroom floor, knowing too well how creaky it is. I kneel at my dresser and reach my hand under. I feel the envelope and rip it from the bottom of the drawer. I fold it and stuff it in my pocket.

I hear a car honking outside. It sounds like it's coming from down the road. Thinking it's a car alarm, I peek out the window. I see the headlights flicker on and off from our car and realize it's Brent honking the horn. I look down at the driveway.

Benson's car is back!

I have two minutes to get out. I can't let Brent come inside.

Benson steps out, staggers, and slams the door. He trips and falls into one of the garbage cans that are always sitting outside the door. I hear the metal clink and him swear as he kicks one garbage can into another. They tip over and spill garbage on the driveway.

He spits and swears, staggers again, then disappears through the front door.

He's drunk. Maybe he'll go straight to the couch and pass out. I look at my watch and step lightly back across the room and behind the door. Through the crack, I watch Benson as he kicks off his shoes, stumbling over as the side table he's leaning on wobbles and tips.

He swears and kicks the table.

I hold my breath.

He walks up the stairs. I almost cry with relief when he goes into the bathroom.

I step out of my old bedroom and cross the bathroom. The door is open a few inches. My steps are quick and heavy. *I'm down to about ninety seconds until Brent comes in. I don't have time for gentle steps.*

"Crystal," Benson booms from the bathroom.

My heart stops.

"Get me a beer," he says.

I freeze.

"Crystal," he yells louder.

I need to shut him up so Crystal doesn't come out and find me. "Yeah, whatever," I say to the door, in the best impersonation of my mother than I can manage.

He's drunk enough that he doesn't even notice. I breathe a little sigh of relief and go down the stairs, forcing myself not to run. When I reach the bottom step, the bathroom door creaks open. *Figures the pig doesn't even flush the toilet or wash his hands.*

I stop, frozen in place like a deer in headlights. I keep my back to him. "I'll bring it right up," I say, "just give a second." Again, I try to sound cranky and crusty, like my mom.

I hear his footsteps move across the hall. *He's coming toward me.* I start walking, past the kitchen and toward the door.

"You missed the kitchen," he snarls.

"What?" I look up and then trip on one of his shoes that have landed in the middle of the room. I grab onto the wall for balance.

When I look up, he's half running, half falling down the stairs.

"Danny?" he sounds surprised.

I'm the one surprised. Surprised he even recognized me when he's obviously very drunk.

"Get back here," he says.

I start to run toward the door. I reach for it and turn.

It's locked!

The extra two seconds I take to turn the deadbolt is all he needs to catch me. I scream as he takes a handful of my hair and pulls me toward him.

"What is that?" he yells when he looks down at my belly. "You think you can just run off and get pregnant and then come back for me to take care of your brat?" he sneers. "I guess I'll have to teach you another lesson."

I close my eyes and brace myself for the blow, covering as much of my belly as I can with my arms.

It doesn't come. Instead, there is a loud crash. When I open my eyes, I see Brent's body on top of Benson's on the back porch. They have crashed through the glass patio door.

I scream and look for something to use as a weapon. Benson's baseball bat is by the front door. I grab it and run to them. They're rolling around, fists are flying, they're both swearing and yelling at each other. I raise the bat, ready to swing. Just as I'm about to swing at Benson, they flop over again, and Brent is on top. I hold my swing.

"What's going on?" my mom screams, running toward us.

The sound of her voice startles both Brent and me, and in the second we both take to look at her, Benson has grabbed the side table and is smashing it against Brent's head. "No!" I scream. I start kicking Benson, who has pushed Brent off him and is trying to stand up.

I swing the bat and hit him again and again. He just laughs at me. He's eyes are glassy and he's spitting, practically foaming at the mouth.

He grabs the bat from me and hits Brent in the head, across the chest, straight down on the nose. He's busted up and blood is pouring out of him. I'm screaming. Crystal is screaming.

I dig around, looking for something else to use against Benson. Brent is no longer moving. *I have to kill Benson.* That is the only thought I have when I find a hunting knife in a drawer. I turn to Benson; he's stopped hitting Brent and has the bat raised to me.

I squeeze the knife as he takes a step toward me. "Time to get rid of this baby, too, and get you back to work," he says and takes another step toward me. He swings the bat and it hits me across the upper arm.

I fall back but keep hold of the knife. I take a step forward and swing the knife, but he steps back, and I miss. He swings again, and I turn so that the bat hits me in the hip. I fall to my knees and look up at him. I've dropped the knife. I have nothing else to fight with. But I will not cry for him. If he's going to kill me, he'll have to look me in the eyes as he takes his final swing.

I'm staring up at him as he raises the bat. Then I hear a loud shot and Benson falls to the ground. I look up behind me, stunned. Crystal is standing there, both hands raised and gripping a gun. She looks at me, looks down at Brent and then Benson. She takes a step toward Benson and unloads three more bullets into his face.

She drops to her knees, covering her face with one hand while the other dangles at her side, still clutching the gun, and lets out the most tortured, gut-wrenching cry I have ever heard.

I crawl to Brent. He's not moving. I bend over him, trying to find a pulse, but there is none. My head is on his chest. My fingers are on his neck. There is nothing. "No!" I scream. "No!" I throw my body on top of his. *Please be alive. Please be alive,* I beg over and over.

There's a commotion at the door and I hear people running inside. Police sirens blare in the background. I look up to the front door and I think I must be dead, because the only face I see is Elly's.

We stare at each other for a moment and then we both jump when we hear a loud shot.

I turn to look and see our mother, sprawled crookedly on the floor. Elly runs to her. My mother's face is twisted and pained, and blood is squirting from her head. The gun is still clutched between her lifeless fingers.

CHAPTER 22

Elaina

"Leave her alone!" I scream as I jump off the top bunk and onto the monster's back. I wrap my legs around its waist and grab onto its shoulders with my fists. The monster freezes for a moment, long enough to let Annie escape its grip. She rolls off her bed and lands on the floor with a thud. She yelps in pain and grabs her ankle.

The monster raises its hands over its back and grabs me by the hair. It leans forward as it pulls me over its shoulders and tosses me on the bed, filling up the spot where Annie was just seconds earlier.

Her pillow feels warm against my cheek and I think for a moment that her bed is more comfortable than mine. I'd like to curl up and take a nap.

But the monster is still there. I can't sleep now. It's coming for me. It leans into me, breathing hot, stinky breath into my face and burning my nostrils. Its pupils are large, and its eyes are bloodshot. Sweat drips from its hairy face and a drop lands on my forehead, stinging my skin. I start to cry out, but I stop myself. I don't want it to know that it's hurt me. Its teeth are rotten and white gobs of spit are pooled in the corners of its mouth. It's frothing like it's a rabid animal.

I turn from it, trying to escape the awful smell and sight of it. I see Annie, crawling across the room, her pyjama bottoms slippery on the wood floor. She stops and crouches in a corner, still holding her ankle. Our eyes meet and we stare at each other in the moonlight. There is fear in her eyes. I've never seen her afraid before, it throws me off. I don't know how to react. She's the strong one. She keeps me safe. She's not afraid of anything. Or is she?

"You," the monster shouts into my face, drawing out the word. "You will take her place."

"No!" I yell and lift my legs to try to kick at it. It moves toward me and my foot connects with its chin. It howls and growls. Bares its teeth and raises its arm to swing at me.

"Don't touch her!" Annie yells. She's up and running across the room toward the monster.

"Annie, no!" I shout. I want her to run the other way. I want her to run out the door and be safe from the monster.

The monster stumbles and falls on me as Annie jumps on its back. I can't breathe. It's squishing me. I squirm and twist and try to get out from beneath it. It twists and shakes, knocking Annie off its back. It picks her up and throws her across the room. I watch her body crumple as she hits the wall so hard the window shakes and I'm afraid it will break, spewing shards of glass on top of her. The monster stands there, in the middle of the room, looking back and forth between us. Its chest is heaving, and fog is shooting from its mouth with its quick, heavy breaths. It's shifting its glance between us, like it's doing an "eenie, meenie, miney, mo" count in its head, trying to decide which one of us to go after.

"Take me," Annie whispers.

The monster immediately leaps toward her, lifts her limp body under his arms and carries her in the crook of his elbow. It stomps across the bedroom floor. At the doorway, the monster pauses. Annie looks up and our eyes meet. Her eyes are empty, hollow. She doesn't fight, she doesn't cry. She just stares at me as the monster carries her away.

"No!" I scream. I try to run after her, but my legs won't move. "Nnn—" I try to scream again, but my voice catches in my throat.

I'm tangled in the blankets, I can't move. I try to shove the blankets off me, but they are twisting, tightening around my arms, pulling me back into the bed.

I watch, frozen in horror, as the monster disappears with my sister out of our room and down the stairs.

Finally, my cry is released, and I howl, begging the monster to bring my sister back to me.

"Laney. Laney!" Something's calling me. It's shaking me. The monster's back.

"No," I fight. It's dark, I can't see. I swing my fists blindly.

"Laney, it's me, it's Dad." He keeps shaking me.

I feel my fist connect.

"Oh!" Dad shouts.

I open my eyes and search the room.

"You're dreaming," he says. "It's just a dream. You fell asleep watching TV."

I had just gotten home earlier that morning, at the end of my first semester. Dad had thought I should take the day to rest, then we would talk about looking for Annie tomorrow.

He's got both his hands covering his nose. I see blood drip between them, so I grab a box of tissues.

"I'm so sorry, Dad," I cry.

"It's okay," he says, "you were having a nightmare."

"No," I say, the fear returning. "It's Annie. She needs me." I try to push him aside and get out of bed.

I'm in my house. I'm safe. There is no monster in here.

He presses his hands onto my shoulders, trying to hold me down. "You fell asleep watching a movie. What were you watching?" he looks at the TV. "It was just a dream, honey. It was just a dream," he says, rubbing my back and turning his attention back to me.

"No," I say firmly. "It was a warning. Annie needs me. I'm going to get her, with or without you. I'm leaving right now."

"There," I say, pointing to the side of the road. The little blue dot on my phone shows that we are close. "Park here," I say. There are cars parked along both sides of the road, some with empty spaces in between. We pull into one of the available spots. I look at the number on the house closest to us then look two houses away. "It's there," I say. "That house right there."

It is the strangest feeling to look at a house that I know I started my life in, and that I now also know held a monster that hurt my sister, but that I have absolutely no recollection of.

I'm opening the door before he has stopped the car.

"Wait a second," Dad says, tugging on my sleeve. "You can't run over there ready for a fight. You don't even know if she lives there."

"We'll find her here," I say. "I just know it." I feel it in my heart. She's close.

"Then we'll both go," he says.

"No," I say. "I need to do this alone."

"Why?"

"Maybe she's afraid of you," I suggest. "Maybe you scared her that day in the park. You can't scare her again."

We both look up, startled, as a car squeals out of the driveway from the house we are looking at. *Annie's house.* It backs up quickly, stops just inches from our car, and takes off, kicking dirt and little stones up at the car. They ping as they bounce off the metal fender.

I push the door open again and start to climb out.

"I don't even know for sure if this is the right house," Dad admits. He's looking at the house and shaking his head slightly. He rubs his forehead.

"What do you mean?" I ask, dropping back into my seat.

"Well . . ." he says. He scratches his head and looks away.

I wait, staring at him.

"After we left the park you pointed to this house as we walked by. But you were three years old. I don't know for sure if you really recognized it as your house or not. You were three. You could have pointed to any house that just reminded you of yours. As soon as you pointed at it, I picked you up and got you to cover your face. I started running. I might not have even come back to the right house when I returned to check the address."

I stare at the house, trying to force myself to find some stored memory deep within my mind.

A car pulls into an empty spot across the road from us. A woman climbs out, then leans back through the open window to talk to the driver.

"So, Annie might not even know I'm looking for her?" I feel rage grow inside me. "All this time, I've been waiting for her to write us back, to call, and we may have sent it to the wrong address? How could you do this to me?"

"You were having nightmares—you needed reassurance. You needed hope. It was all I had. Maybe it's the right house. Maybe she received the letter. I don't know. I'm sorry." He's looking around, at me, at the house, at the cars around us. His eyes are wide; he's on alert. He looks like a caged animal trying to find an escape route.

"Didn't you check? After you took me, I mean, didn't you follow the news story? Weren't you interested in the family you took me from?" I ask.

I look back at the car across the street and notice that the woman is gone. The man in the driver's seat is watching her walk down the road. She's walking funny, a sort of slow waddle, with one hand holding her back. She cuts across the yard, leaving footprints in the snow-covered lawn and disappears into the house we're watching.

My old house?

"There was no story," Dad says quietly.

"What? What are you talking about?" I forget about the woman and the house.

"I tried. I watched the news every single day, I read every newspaper I could find. I was afraid every single second that someone would come looking for you. But there was never any mention of a missing child. There was nothing. No news story, no police searching. Nothing."

"Nobody even cared that I was gone?" I ask.

"I'm sure they cared," Dad says. His words mean nothing, though.

"Nobody looked for me?" I sink back into my chair. I feel like a baby bird plucked from its nest by the hands of an inquisitive child. "My mother didn't even look for me?" *She just went on with her life like nothing had happened? Never looked for me? Never called the police? Was I that bad of a kid that she didn't even try to get me back?*

"I'm sorry," he says.

I sit, staring ahead. The same car that pulled out just minutes earlier is back. I watch it pull into the driveway, but it doesn't register. I have only one thought: *No one looked for me. No one cared to try to get me back.*

Annie sent me away. My mother didn't look for me. Maybe I was better off without any of them. No, my mind struggles, *Annie sent me away to protect me because she loved me. She needs me now.*

A car honking brings me back from my thoughts. I whip around, looking for the source of the noise. It's the car across the street from us. The driver is pressing down again and again on the horn and blinking the lights. He's staring at the same house we're watching. He looks frantic. He's sitting up in his seat, almost climbing on top of the steering wheel.

I watch the man, still dazed from what my father just told me, until he leaps from his car and runs across the yard to the house.

Why is everyone going to this house right now?

I try to pull up a memory of my mother. *Nothing.* I can't picture her face. I don't remember her touch. I can't recall one moment of time with her. Then I see Annie's face. I see us skipping down the road; she's holding my hand as we skip. She was always holding my hand. She was always looking out for me.

There, finally! I see the house in my mind, years ago, when it was freshly painted and there was a garden in the front yard. Our bedroom window above the driveway used to have a giant pink construction paper butterfly taped to it. Annie had cut it out then she let me help her decorate it. She taped it up to the window so that I would always know which house was ours when we were on our way home from the park. We always stopped skipping when we got to this house and stood, staring up at the butterfly. Annie would lean down and whisper into my ear, "Don't be afraid, Elly, I'll protect you." She would squeeze my hand and keep it in hers and we walked slowly up the driveway and disappeared through the front door.

"That's the house," I say. I stare up at the bedroom window, my old bedroom window. The butterfly is gone, but it's the same window. "I'm sure of it."

Dad and I are both looking at the house when a loud gunshot goes off. We both jump. *Annie!* I open the door and jump out. I run across the lawn. I hear screaming coming from inside the house. "Annie! I'm coming, Annie!" I yell. I slip on a patch of ice underneath the snow and fall. I roll and tumble across the yard, landing on my back. I notice the sky looks dark. *Another warning?*

"Laney! Wait!" Dad is yelling behind me. He catches me and helps me up. He's trying to check me over, to make sure I'm okay, but I brush him off and start running again toward the house.

Three more gunshots ring through my ears. *Oh my God!*

There's a scream. The awful, tortured cry of an animal being devoured alive.

I push through the front door and I see her. She's crouched on the floor, cowering. She's covered in blood. Her hair is matted and wet. She's not moving. *Is she dead?*

I hold my breath. I will never forgive myself if she's dead.

She screams and moves; her body shakes like she's crying and she flings her arms out and on top of the body lying on the floor. I let out a sigh of relief. *She's alive. Is it her?*

There's another body lying on the floor. Blood is gushing out of holes in the forehead and cheeks. My body freezes the instant I look at the face. *The monster.*

There's another person, sitting up, beside that body. She's alive, I can tell, but I know right away that it's not Annie, so I look away, back to the woman crouching on the floor.

Dad trips and falls into a table beside the door.

The woman moves again, raises her head and looks at me.

I stare at her and our eyes lock. *It's her. It's Annie. She's alive.*

I jump when another gunshot pierces the air. I see a body from the corner of my eye crumple to the ground. I run to the woman, peer down at her. Blood and brain matter are pouring from her ear. I look into her lifeless eyes and I know I am looking into the face of my mother.

CHAPTER 23

Danica

"Annie . . ." I feel my body shaking slightly. "Annie . . ." The voice calling me is soft and musical, like a dream fairy. *I'm dreaming,* I think, even as I open my eyes and see the most beautiful sight I've ever seen.

"Elly?" I whisper, my voice hoarse and crackly. I try to get up. My head is spinning. I squint to try to block out the bright light that is shining above me. Machines are beeping all around me. Her face is like an angel's. The light is glowing around her hair, causing it to look like she has a halo above her head. Her eyes are big and bright.

"No," she says, putting her hands on my shoulders, "stay down, you need your rest." She leans into me and my face disappears under her cascade of hair. It smells of flowers and spring and life.

"Oh, Annie," she cries as her body shakes. "I'm so happy we found you in time."

"What— what happened?" I ask. I'm trying to draw up a memory, but my head is foggy. I look around and see the machines that are beeping at me. "Where am I?"

"You're in the hospital. You've been unconscious for two days," she says. "The doctors have been taking good care of you here," she says.

A pain shoots through my hip and I remember. I flinch as I see Benson swing the bat at me, aiming for my belly. I had covered my belly and turned, giving him my hip instead to beat with his bat.

"My baby," I remember, suddenly afraid. I reach down and feel my belly. It's still huge. I choke out a sigh of relief. I spread my fingers across both sides, waiting to feel a kick. There's nothing. "My baby," I say again, my eyes wide with fear as I try once again to get up.

"Your baby is fine," Elly says. "Stay down and rest. Your baby is just fine."

A man—George, I remember his name from his letter—comes up beside Elly and places his arm around her, resting his hand on her shoulder. *He's still protecting her,* I notice and smile. He looks exactly the same as he had in the park all those years ago, with just a few extra wrinkles and a few grey hairs.

I feel the baby stretch out and kick me in the ribs. A little lump distends out from my belly from the baby's foot or elbow. Relief floods through me and I feel tears pool in my eyes. My baby's okay. I wrap my arms around my belly in a hug and relax, thankful. And then another memory seizes me. *Brent. Dead. Benson killed him.*

"Brent," I say. "I need to see Brent." I rip one wire from the back of my hand and another that had been attached to my chest.

Elly looks startled.

The machines respond with louder beeps. "Where is he?" I cry. I know the answer, but I don't want to hear it.

"No. No," I cry out, in a high-pitched, strangled voice as Elly lowers and shakes her head.

"I'm so sorry, Annie," she says. She wipes her eyes with her sleeve, but it doesn't catch all her tears. "I'm sorry."

George squeezes her to him, and he puts his other hand on my shoulder. "Annie, I'm sorry," he says, barely above a whisper, "Brent didn't make it."

"No! No!" I wail as the beeping from the machine grows even louder, piercing my thoughts and making me want to smash the machines. Two nurses rush in, pushing Elly and her dad away from my bed. One grabs my arm as the other plunges a needle under my skin.

I need to get out of here. I need to find Brent.

I continue fighting them until my muscles stop listening to me and I fall back onto my bed, angry that my body is not responding to my commands. My eyelids feel heavy, my heart is broken. So, I give in to the urge to sleep and I willingly plunge into the darkness that is buried so deep inside my heart.

When I feel the heaviness lift, I blink my eyes open again. I see Elly sitting on a chair by my bed; her knees are pulled up against her chest and her head is resting on them.

I stretch my hand out to her.

She raises her head and jumps out of her chair, reaching her hands out and clasping them around mine. She sits on my bed beside me. Her eyes are red and puffy.

I see her father standing in the doorway, talking to a doctor. When he looks over and sees me awake, he says something quickly to the doctor then comes inside and sits down on my bed, opposite Elly.

"They're going to release you tomorrow," he says, "and you are going to come home with us."

I shake my head. "No," I say. *I don't want to be a bother.*

"Don't," Elly says. "Please don't fight us, Annie. Please come home with us. I need you to come home with us."

"Brent," I say weakly.

"His body has been released to his parents," George says. "The funeral is in two days. We will take you if you want to go."

I nod.

"I'm sorry," George says. He squeezes my hand. "I'm so sorry, Annie. I should have taken both of you home with me, that day in the park. I didn't know. I won't make that mistake again. I won't ever leave you again."

I look at Elly. *What is he talking about?* I ask her with my eyes.

"The doctors had to examine you," she explains. "To make sure everything was okay with the baby. You were unconscious for two days." She's looking at me like I'm a sad, broken little porcelain doll. "They had to be sure the baby was okay." Her words catch in her throat as she talks.

I turn my face away, my cheeks burning with embarrassment. *Does she know? Do they both know?* Shame envelops me and I wish the bed would open up and swallow me whole. I want to be anywhere in the world at that moment other than at the receiving end of their pity.

So, I go away. I feel myself leave my body and float above them. The pain disappears. The shame disappears. All that's left is a feeling of nothingness. A welcome, comforting, empty feeling that I know so well.

I watch them, lean over me, concerned about me. I hear them. I hear Elly's awful words. "You have two broken ribs, a broken arm and a fractured hand that never healed properly, from when you were little, the doctors said."

I hear her words, but they don't affect me. They don't bring back any memories. They aren't associated with any pain. From where I am right now, nothing can hurt me.

I watch Elly place her hand on my belly.

My baby. I can't feel my baby, I realize in a panic. *I have to return. I can't escape the feelings of shame and embarrassment if it means I have to give up feeling my baby, also. I need my baby, the only piece of Brent that I have left.*

So I return. I feel myself back in my body. I see them looking at me. I feel the shame burn in my cheeks from what Benson has done to me, what I let him do to me.

"You have burns, cigarette burns they think, and cuts all over your body."

Now her words bring pain. I remember each cigarette that sizzled and burned deep into my skin. I feel the release of pain and see the bright red blood appear with each razor I forced into my own skin.

"And scarring," she continues, "on the inside. Lots of scarring. The doctors said there is so much internal damage that they were surprised you had been able to conceive."

I look away. I can't face her. I can't let her know what I am.

"The monster was real, wasn't he?" she asks.

When I keep my face turned away from her, she starts singing. "Go away, monster, I'm not afraid of you. I'll make you go away, I know what to do. I keep my eyes closed and sing my song. And when I wake up, you'll be gone."

My heart stops and my body shakes. When I turn to look at her I'm expecting tears, but she's not crying. She's looking at me with admiration and love. "You taught me that song, didn't you, Annie?"

I nod.

"Is that why you told me to take her that day in the park?" George asks. "Is that why you made me promise to keep her safe?"

I nod.

"Oh, Annie," Elly cries. She throws her body over mine. "I'm sorry. I'm so sorry. I didn't know. I didn't remember. I forgot about you for so long. I left you all alone with the monster." She's wailing now, a high-pitched scream that sends a pain shooting through my brain.

"I didn't know either," George says. "I should have taken both of you. I thought I was doing the wrong thing. I took a child to ease my own pain, to ease my wife's pain for the child we had lost. I told myself it was okay because we would take care of the child. That no matter what home life we were talking her from, we would make her new life even better. I told myself that her parents would be sad, they would miss her, but they would still have one child to take care of. It wasn't fair. My wife and I had lost our only child. We had no one left. Other parents had lots of kids. More than they could handle. Your parents sent the two of you off to the park alone. I told myself they didn't deserve to keep both of you, that they weren't good parents if they let you both go out alone when you were so young. But I never thought, I never imagined, that I was leaving you to a life of abuse. I never . . . I didn't know. I would have taken you, too. I would have helped you."

Both of them, Elly and her father, are crying and shaking and dripping snot all over my bed sheets. I start to laugh at the craziness of it, at the cruel joke fate had played on all of us. My laughter quickly turns to tears, and the three of us cry together, huddled in a heap, until our tears wash away the years.

CHAPTER 24

Elaina

"You have to go back to school," Dad says.

"There is no way I'm leaving her," I say.

"Christmas break is over, you have to go back. Norman is going to be here to pick you up any minute."

"I'll transfer schools," I say. "I'll live at home and go to school."

"What if you can't transfer?" Dad says. "There's a process to follow. You have to apply. You need to finish out your year."

"I'm not leaving her, Dad, no matter what anyone says. I don't care if I lose the year of school. I don't care if I have to start over. I don't care about anything except being here to take care of Annie."

The doorbell rings.

"And no one is going to force me to," I say, turning to get the door and preparing myself for another fight. I haven't told Norman yet, although I'm hopeful that he'll just know that I can't leave Annie.

"You ready?" Norman asks when I open the door.

Seriously? Does no one understand me at all?

"I'm not going back," I say. I turn and see Dad watching us, so I step outside and pull the door closed behind me.

"What?" Norman asks. "You have to come back."

"No, I don't," I say. "Annie needs me."

"I'm only going to this school so I could be with you," he says. "It wasn't even in my top five, I only agreed because you wanted to go there."

"I'm sorry," I say, "I can't go back. I can't leave her. She needs me."

"I need you, too," he says, sulking. It's so unattractive.

"She's going to need my help when the baby comes," I say. "I have to stay. I have to help her with the baby."

"What about me?" he asks.

"I'll see you when you come home. I'm going to transfer schools, live at home and just take classes nearby."

"Just like that? You've changed all our plans. Without even talking to me about it?"

"Maybe you can transfer, too," I suggest.

"My parents won't let me transfer. I had to fight them to get them to pay for this program. They were mad when I turned down the football scholarship and said I was going to the same school as you."

"I'm sorry," I say.

"That's it?" he asks.

"I have to help Annie with the baby," I say.

"What about our plans, Laney? What about our wedding? What about our kids one day?"

I shrug.

"We had a plan, Laney. What if I don't want a ready-made family? What if I don't want to give up my plans to take care of someone else's baby?"

I don't understand what happened to the Norman I thought I knew so well. He would have known without me having to speak a word. He would know that I could never leave Annie again.

"Will you talk to me?" he pleads. "You told me four weeks ago that you found your sister, she's pregnant and that you and your dad brought her home. Then you refused to see me for the last four weeks. You didn't even come to my family's Christmas dinner."

"I don't have time for this," I say.

"Just talk to me, Laney, I don't understand what's going on. What has changed?"

"Annie's here," I say.

"Yes, you said that," he replies.

"And she's pregnant."

"Yep, you said that, too. That's about all you've said."

He sounds so whiny right now. I don't have time to explain; Annie is upstairs and she needs me. I want to run back upstairs and be with her. I need to make up for all the time we lost. I need to somehow show her how much I love her and make up for all the pain she experienced because she was trying to protect me.

"Why can't she take care of her own baby?" he asks.

"I won't force you, but I need to do this, Norman. If you don't understand, then you obviously don't know me at all." I twist the ring and pull it off my finger. "I'm sorry," I say as I hand the ring to him.

He looks confused at first as he looks down at the ring in his open palm. Then his brow furrows and he looks angry. "You can't do this," he says.

"I'm sorry," I say again. I turn around and disappear back inside, closing the door in the face of the man I love and the future we had planned together.

As I race back upstairs to Annie, I see Dad slip out the front door.

CHAPTER 25

Danica

I roll over and just listen to the morning songs of the birds outside. Rays of sunlight burst through my window and dance across my bed. There are pictures of Elly all over the room. Her toothless grin as a young girl framed on the wall, a picture of her and Norman holding hands stuck into the corner of her dresser mirror, a picture of her with her dad and mom, the three of them smiling happily into the camera.

Elly had insisted I take her room and she moved into the guest room when they brought me home from the hospital. I told her I would take the guest room, but she had insisted. This room is warm, it's safe, I can feel Elly in it. *It's a good place for my baby,* I think and place my hands protectively over my baby. "Do you want to live here?" I whisper to my belly. The baby stretches and kicks in response. "Me, too," I whisper.

I imagine Elly growing up here. I can see George tucking her into bed at night, telling her stories, keeping her safe. I remember all the nights I cried myself to sleep, my heart aching for my little sister. The only way I could protect her back then had been to give her away, to send her off with a stranger, not knowing whether I would ever see her again. Not knowing whether the life I was sending her to would be better or worse than the one I was trying to protect her from. *I'm stronger now,* I think, rubbing my belly. "I promise I will protect you," I whisper to my baby.

Although my heart aches for Brent, I feel comfort in the feeling of his baby growing inside me. *The baby I shouldn't have been able to conceive,* the doctors believed. I feel Brent's strength in the baby's legs when it kicks. I feel Brent's love when the baby stretches inside me, like it's giving me a hug from inside, enveloping me in its essence. *If you're a boy, I'll name you after your father,* I think as I watch a wave float across my belly.

"Knock, knock," George says as his knuckles tap on my door.

"I'm awake," I say.

He opens the door. He's carrying a glass of orange juice and a plate with buttered toast. "Hungry?" he asks.

"A little."

Max yips, races past him and hops up on my bed.

I giggle as he licks my face.

"Max, down," George commands.

"He's okay." I laugh. "I like him up here."

He places the glass and plate on the table beside me.

"George," I say when he turns to leave. He stops and turns to me. "I—I just wanted to say thanks."

"No need," he says.

"I really appreciate you letting me stay here. But I don't want to overstay my welcome. I can start looking for my own place. I can get a job. I don't want to be a burden to you."

"Nonsense," he says. He walks back to me and kneels by my bedside, takes my hand into his. "You gave me the greatest gift," he says. "You gave me Laney. You gave up a piece of your heart in order to protect her. At five years old you understood more about selfless love than most people understand in their entire lives. I could never repay you for that, and I just left you there. I didn't even check up on you. I was so filled with relief when I didn't see any stories about a missing child, that I didn't even stop for a moment to wonder why that was. To think about what type of home I had left you in if no one even noticed a little girl missing from it. I should have checked in on you. If you ever need anything, anything at all, just say the words." He squeezes my hand and leans over me, placing a kiss on my forehead.

"George," I say as he turns to leave again. "There is actually something I need from you."

One morning, a week later, after I shower, I dress and head downstairs to watch television. I turn on Dr. Phil, my favourite. He's talking to a teenage girl who's crying. She looks so sad and pathetic. She has the same dead look in her eyes that I saw in my own reflection most of my life. I flip the channel quickly and settle on a cooking show. I rub my belly as I watch, trying to rub away the cramping that I feel.

A little while later Elly comes in and sits beside me. "How's the baby?" she asks.

"All good." I smile. "How was class?"

"It was okay, kinda boring actually. You ready for your Lamaze class? We have to leave in ten minutes."

"Yep, just have to pee. Again." I laugh as I get up.

We practice breathing through class and at the end the leader tells us that next week's class will involve a trip to the hospital. "It's getting close," Elly whispers. "Are you getting scared?"

"I'm excited," I say. "I can't wait to hold him in my arms."

"Him?"

"Or her." I laugh. "Sometimes I picture a little boy, just like Brent." I shrug. "I am a little afraid, actually," I admit, "of not feeling Brent inside me anymore. What if I start to forget about him once the baby's out?"

"You'll never forget him," Elly says. "You'll think about him every time you look into your baby's eyes."

"How'd you get so smart?" I ask.

"I must take after my sister," she says, nudging me in the arm.

"Thank you for being my coach," I say. "I don't want to have to go in there alone."

"You're never alone," she says. "You'll never be alone again." She takes my hand and holds it as we walk back to the car.

She opens my door for me and I lean to get inside. "Ow," I moan, rubbing my hip. "What's wrong?" she asks. She's right by my side, leaning into the car.

"My hip. I just twisted funny, I think. It's still tender sometimes. I'm okay," I reassure her. She watches me for a second, then turns to leave.

A sharp pain shoots across my stomach and I yell out in pain. "What?" she says, back at my side. "What is it?"

"My stomach," I say.

"Contraction?"

"I don't know. Maybe."

"Oh my God," she says. "Okay. Just relax. It's okay." She's starting to hyperventilate.

"You relax," I tease. "I'm the one having a baby here. You're supposed to be the calm one. What did we take all these classes for anyway?" I laugh.

"Okay." She takes a deep breath in. "You're right." She lets her breath out slowly. "I'm calm. I'm calm."

"Ow," I say again as I'm jolted with another pain.

"Contraction." She nods as she pulls out her phone and checks the time. "Let's wait, see if you have another one. I have to time it."

I sit back and close my eyes, keeping my hands moving across my stomach.

I shout out when I feel another pain. "That was only five minutes," she says. "We have to go to the hospital."

"But I don't have a bag ready," I say. "It's not time. I'm not ready." I'm shaking my head. "We have to go home. Ow!"

"It sounds like the baby is ready." She laughs. "Hold on." She taps into her phone and I hear it ring. "Dad," she says into the phone. "The baby's coming. I'm taking Annie to the hospital.

Meet us there. You need to pack a bag for her and bring it with you. Remember the diapers, and some baby clothes, and—"

"I've done this before, you know." I hear him through the phone.

"Oh yes, right, okay," she says and taps the screen again then puts the phone in her pocket. She starts and car and pauses, looks over at me and takes my hand. "You ready for this?" she asks.

I nod, fear racing through me.

She puts the car in gear, and we drive off.

"Do you have to hit every bump?" I ask, as the car bounces over yet another pothole.

"I'm sorry," she says, "the roads are crappy. I can't help it. I'll slow down."

"No," I yell, as another wave of pain ripples through me. "Just get me to the hospital." *I can't take the pain.*

"Breathe," Laney says. "Deep breaths, just like in class."

Right, breathe, I think and take a deep breath in just like we learned. I let it out slowly. *Yes, this is good.* Another pain shoots through me. "Ow!" I yell.

"Focus. Breathe," she's instructing me. She reaches over to me and grabs my hand.

"Just watch the road," I yell, pulling my hand away from hers.

"Okay," she says, "we're here. I'm pulling up to the hospital now." The car slows as she pulls up to the front doors. She jumps out of the car and comes around, helping me out.

"Aren't you going to move it?" I ask, turning around to look at the car. I double over as another contraction hits.

"No," she says. "They can give me a ticket, I have to get you inside."

I holler and scream like a mad woman as Elly gives my information. A nurse comes over with a wheelchair and I gladly sit in it. Elly follows as the nurse pushes me into a room. "Help her get into this gown," the nurse says.

After a minor wrestling match, I'm in the gown and lying on a bed. Elly jumps each time I yell out in pain. "Breathe," she repeats over and over.

I try the breathing. "The stupid breathing doesn't work," I snarl after another contraction overtakes me. "Get me something," I beg.

Elly runs out and comes back with a nurse. "You're eight centimetres," the nurse says after she examines me. "It's almost time."

They wheel me into another room, and we're followed in by tons of people in scrubs.

"Do you want gas?" a young nurse asks. "For the pain?" she says when I look at her blankly.

I nod.

She rolls a tank over and hands me the nose cover. "Put this over your mouth and nose and take a deep breath in," she says.

I do as she says and take three fast deep breaths. A fog takes over, which feels amazing. I start to laugh, quietly at first, which quickly becomes hysterical giggling. I suck in another burst of gas and laugh some more. It feels great. I feel fantastic.

Another contraction hits.

"Ooooowwww!" I scream. I'm shouting over and over. I'm trying to get up, off the bed, to run away from the pain. I'm sweating profusely and I feel like all my hair is stuck to my face. I see a pregnant woman stop in the doorway. Our eyes meet as I scream out in pain once more. She looks petrified. I must look like a rabid animal being tortured.

The pain subsides and I take another few hits of gas. *Ah, yes.* I start hysterical giggling again.

I feel a gush of liquid and I yell out, "I'm peeing."

"Your water just broke," Elly says to me, leaning in so that her mouth is practically touching my ear.

I moan again as another contraction starts. I start to push. "Not yet," the nurse admonishes. "Not yet."

I take another hit of gas, giggle and then push again with the next contraction.

"Not yet," the nurse says. She bends down and puts her face right in my face. "Look at me," she instructs.

I look, but I can't focus. My eyes are blurry. My head feels foggy.

"If you won't listen to me, I will have to take the gas away," she threatens.

"I'm listening. I'm listening," I say. I look right at her, but there's two of her. My eyes are crossed. I can't straighten them. I start to giggle again.

"It's not time to push yet, Annie," she says. "I'll tell you when to push, but it's not time yet. You're not ready."

Another contraction pulsates through me and I scream in her face, "I'm pushing!" I lift the gas mask to my face and take another deep breath.

"Stop pushing," she says, taking the mouth cover from my hand. My fist is squeezed tight around it and she has to fight me to get it.

"Epidural," I say.

"It's too late," she says. "I'm sorry. It's almost time, you're almost ready."

"Breathe, Annie," Elly says, "just breathe. Come on, I'll do it with you." She overemphasizes sucking in a breath, watching me, waiting for me to follow.

I'm seized by another shooting pain. It's ripping through me. *I can't take it. I can't take the pain.* I think about Elly as a little girl. I'm pushing her on a swing. "Higher!" She giggles, so I grab hold of the swing and run underneath her, giving her an underdoggy. She soars high into the air. The pain is gone. I can't feel anything but the wind as I run under her swing. The voices of the nurses and machines are gone and all I hear is Elly's laughter. *Yes, this is better*, I think. *No more pain, just me and Elly.*

I see myself, lying on the table, Elly holding my hand beside me. She's leaning over and talking to me but I can't hear her words. I see my face, distorted in pain, crying out for help, but I feel nothing. I just float, above myself, biding my time until it's safe to come back, until the pain is gone, and I can return to my body.

My baby, I think. *Brent.* I don't want to miss this. I don't want to disappear from this pain. I will myself back and feel myself re-enter my body. The pain has changed. Now it's making me feel alive. I can do this. I want this. This is good pain. I need to feel this; I want to remember every moment of it.

I feel Elly's hand in mine again and I watch her. She's so strong and brave. She's everything I hoped she would be. And she's safe, that's the most important thing. I had done my job, I had been a good big sister to her. I had kept my promise to our dad.

"Inhale," she instructs me, leaning in close and looking me in the eyes. Our faces are only inches apart. "You can do this," she says. She smiles at me and it is the most beautiful smile I've ever seen.

"We can do this," I correct. With her by my side again, I feel like I can do anything. My life has purpose again.

I listen to her and take a deep breath and then breathe out slowly in unison with her. We repeat again and I feel myself start to calm.

"One more," she says, and we do it again.

It's all going to be okay.

Another sensation sears through me. It feels like something's ripping. I feel like something is being ripped apart inside me. I scream out and sit up. This pain is different than before. I can't handle it. Colours are exploding all around me, like there are fireworks going off in the delivery room. "I can't do this," I shout. "I can't do this!" *I can't take this pain. My body can't handle any more.*

Terror shoots through me. *Something's wrong.*

"Elly," I cry.

"I'm right here, I'm right here," she reassures me. She holds my hand with one hand and strokes my head with the other. Her face is still close to mine.

"There's something wrong," I pant.

She looks at me and my eyes tell her what my words can't.

"Help her!" Elly screams. "Help her! There's something wrong! Do something!"

She looks back at me. "I love you, Annie!" she screams. "Don't leave me! Please don't leave me!"

"I love you, Elly Belly," I whisper. I can't hold on to her hand anymore, so I let go.

She won't let go of my hand and instead wraps her other hand around it, too. She raises it to her face, and I feel her kiss the back of my hand, then she leans in and kisses my cheek.

When she backs away, I see her tears, I see her terror, but I can't do anything about it. This time I feel helpless to protect her from the pain that I know is coming. I can't do anything to protect anyone anymore.

I only have one last wish for my life.

The machines start beeping again. The colours in my mind blend together, muddying my vision. Until all that's left is blackness.

CHAPTER 26

Elaina

I'm looking into Annie's eyes as they roll backwards into her head and she goes limp on the table. "Annie!" I shout.

Machines start crying out, sending a wave of panic through the nurses. One nurse runs out, calling for a doctor. Another nurse pushes in front of me, bumping me out of the way. I'm still holding on to Annie's hand. Her hand is limp in mine, but I can't let go of it. I squat down beside Annie's bed, behind the nurse, and squeeze her hand tightly. *Please be okay, please be okay,* I repeat over and over.

The nurse turns and takes a hold of each of our hands and pulls, separating us. She starts to wheel Annie's bed away.

"No. Wait," I say. "Where are you taking her?"

"We have to go," the nurse says. "There's a problem. She needs a C-section. Now."

"Oh my God. Oh my God. Annie," I cry as she's wheeled out of the room. "Help her. You have to help her." I'm running after them, out of the room and down the hall. They disappear behind a set of doors and I'm stopped when I try to follow.

"Go to the waiting room," a young nurse says. She has kind eyes. I see fear in them.

I grab her arm. "You have to help her," I cry, clutching onto her like I'm on a sinking ship and she's the only lifeboat. "She has to be okay. She has to be okay."

The nurse leads me to a chair and nudges me to sit down. "I'll come get you as soon as I know something," she promises and disappears behind the doors.

"No. No." I'm rocking and moaning. *She has to be okay.*

"Laney. There you are." I look up. It's Dad and Norman. They're running down the hall toward me.

"I'm sorry," Norman says when they reach me. "I'm so sorry for what I said." He sits beside me and puts his arm around my shoulder, pulling me into him. "I didn't know. Why didn't you just tell me?" he asks.

"It doesn't matter," I say. *Nothing matters except Annie.*

I tell them what happened. How the machines went crazy and they took her away. "Emergency C-section," I repeat. "Will she be okay?" I ask. I'm shaking Norman. "She has to be okay!" I yell.

We sit there. And wait. And wait. And wait.

I watch as people walk by. Some carrying gifts, some with balloons. All of them have smiles as they walk toward their loved ones and their new babies. *I hate them. How could they be so happy when my world is falling apart? I just found Annie, I can't lose her. Not now. Not ever.*

I look up and jump out of my chair. A doctor is headed toward us. She must have news. As our eyes meet, I see the news in her eyes. "No!" I yell and try to turn away from her.

Dad and Norman are standing behind me. I try to run, but I bump into them and I'm locked in place. I can't escape the news that I know is coming. I can't run away from the truth that I don't want to hear.

"I'm sorry," the doctor says. "There were complications. Your sister," she says, "the doctors did everything they could. She didn't make it."

"No," I choke out. "Annie," I cry as I crumple to the floor. There is no life left in my legs. There is no reason for my heart to continue beating. I want to curl up and die right there on the floor so that I can join Annie, so that our spirits can be united on the other side. *I didn't have enough time with her. No time would ever be enough.*

"The baby?" Dad asks.

The baby. I'd completely forgotten about the baby. I clutch onto Norman's arm and pull myself back up.

I feel the life pump back into my heart when the doctor's lips curl slightly. "A girl," she says. "She's okay. You can see her shortly."

A girl.

"Would you like me to take you to see Danica now?" she asks. I nod.

She turns and I start to follow. I feel Dad and Norman follow behind me. "Please," I say, turning around and placing a hand up to them in a stop motion. "I need a moment alone with her."

The both nod and stop. I turn to follow the doctor.

She pauses at a doorway and waves me inside. "Take all the time that you need," she says.

I take a deep breath in and step back into the room where she had been, before she was rushed away. It's silent. The machines are no longer beeping. The nurses are no longer running around. The gas tank is no longer hissing. Annie is lying motionless on the bed. Her eyes are closed. Her skin is still pink. She looks like she's sleeping. I watch her, leaning in close. *Breathe,* I urge. I wait. She doesn't listen. She can't.

I throw my body on hers, wrap my arms around her head. There are no words to describe my pain. No way to express the emotions twisting around like a savage tornado inside me. *How do I say goodbye to the sister who saved me? The sister I never even remembered I had until a couple years ago. The sister I owe my life to. She sacrificed herself to save me from the monster. She had the scars to show it. Physical scars. Emotional scars. I bet even her soul was scarred . . . how could it not be? After everything she endured for me, she had still loved me.*

"Annie," I cry into her hair, "please don't leave me. I can't live without you."

I feel the bed shake, the wheels vibrating against the floor as I cry. I pour a lifetime of tears and love into the lifeless body of the sister I love with all my heart, with all my being. I just hold her, I smell her hair, I remember the feel of my arms around her, knowing that when I let go of her this time, that I will be letting go of her forever.

"Knock, knock," Dad says from the doorway. I look up and he's holding a baby, wrapped in a white blanket with pink trim in his arms, Norman standing beside him. "Do you want to hold her?" he asks.

I nod and climb off the bed, leaning in to give Annie one last kiss on her cheek. I pause, knowing this will be the last time I ever see her face again. We had shared a lifetime together, in the few shorts weeks we had together, but it wasn't enough. I want more.

I turn away from Annie for the last time and reach out for the baby. Dad steps toward me and places her in my arms. She fits perfectly into the crook of my elbow. I lean down and give her a kiss on the cheek, imagining all the love I inhaled with the last kiss I placed on her mother's cheek now pouring into her, transferring every ounce of love that had filled Annie's body into this new, beautiful little being.

Norman puts an arm around me as I hold the baby. "I'm sorry," he says. "I didn't mean what I said earlier. We can make anything work. We will make anything work. Please forgive me."

He reaches for my hand that's tucked under the baby and slides my ring back on my finger. "You don't have to give me an answer now, but please think about it," he says. "I didn't know."

"I have to talk to you about something," Dad says. "Danica was afraid something would happen to her in childbirth. She asked me to help her with something," he continues when I look up at him. "She asked me to help her have a will prepared, giving you custody of her baby if anything should happen to her. I told her it wasn't a good idea, that you were too young, but she insisted that she wanted the choice to be yours. She wanted me to tell you that she would understand if you couldn't do it. She didn't want you to know because she didn't want you to worry. But the choice is yours, Laney. It's a big responsibility. You don't have to accept it. You should take some time to think about it."

"I'll take her," I say without a moment's hesitation, looking down at the baby who will be named after her mother. "I'll take Annie," I say, leaning down to kiss her forehead as I squeeze her a little tighter. *There is no question. There is nothing to think about.*

As I hold baby Annie in my arms and gaze into her beautiful newborn face, I see my sister in her. I see her heart and her love. I see everything she sacrificed in her life, all the pain she endured to protect me, because she loved me. I know with all my heart that I will do the same for my sister's baby.

I untuck baby Annie's arm from the blanket and hook her tiny pinky in mine. "I will be everything you need me to be. Your mother, your protector, your guardian. I will do anything for you, Annie," I promise her.

In that moment, Annie opens her eyes and locks her gaze on me, watching me like she can actually understand what I'm saying. I feel her tiny pinky tighten around mine and a tear escapes my eye and falls onto her cheek.

"I would give my life for you, if I had to," I promise her, "just as you mother did for me."

CPSIA information can be obtained
at www.ICGtesting.com
Printed in the USA
BVHW032348060121
597090BV00002B/8